A H[OUSE]
FO[R]
TAKING

BY
AMANDA BROWNING

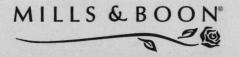

MILLS & BOON®

First published in Great Britain 1997
Harlequin Mills & Boon Limited,
Eton House, 18-24 Paradise Road, Richmond, Surrey TW9 1SR

© Amanda Browning 1997

ISBN 0 263 80171 3

Set in Times Roman 10½ on 11½ pt.
01-9707-53570 C1

Printed and bound in Great Britain
by Mackays of Chatham PLC, Chatham

CHAPTER ONE

TASHA LARSEN thrust her way through the swing doors leading to the hospital's emergency room and strode down the corridor to the desk, her raincoat flapping like wings behind her. She was uncomfortably wet because her cab had been caught in Denver's heavy traffic, and she had abandoned it to walk the last few blocks.

'I was told my sister was brought here. Name of Larsen,' she declared coolly, glad that her demeanour of composed assurance—which stood her in such good stead in the courtroom—hid the anxious beat of her heart. The usually unflappable clerk behind the desk did a double-take, seemed about to make a remark and then, catching sight of Tasha's expression, thought better of it.

'You'll find her in ICU. Take the elevator to the sixth floor.'

ICU? Dear God! Why hadn't she been told that it was that serious? Telling herself not to think the worst, Tasha headed for the elevator—oblivious to the bemused stare of the clerk. When the doors opened on the upper floor she stepped out and looked around. There didn't seem to be anybody to ask, but she was used to making quick decisions and unhesitatingly turned right. Glancing into rooms as she went, she caught sight of a figure she knew and hurried inside.

Far from being motionless in a bed, her sister was pacing up and down the small waiting-room.

'When they said you were in ICU I expected to find you badly injured,' Tasha observed tautly.

5

'Disappointed?' Her sister sent her a mocking look from eyes the same colour as Tasha's own.

In fact, everything about them was the same for Natalya and Natasha Larsen were twenty-seven-year-old identical twins. They were quite breathtakingly beautiful, with eyes of so deep a blue they were almost violet and bones so fine they appeared fragile. Their skin was like porcelain, contrasting magnificently with the black sheen of their hair. Both were tall, willowy and extremely femininely curved.

The only observable difference between them was that Natasha—Tasha for short—had her hair styled in a bob which curved into her neck. The really important differences didn't show. Because of them, the sisters had had a parting of the ways a long time ago.

Natalya was an exceptionally good PA but she used her looks to get what she wanted, rather than her brain. Men, she claimed, thought with a different part of their anatomy and could be controlled by it, getting her the good things in life quickly.

By contrast, Tasha found that her looks worked against her in her work as a lawyer. She had to work doubly hard to convince people that she was more than a pretty face.

Despite the fact that they rarely saw each other—Natalya's choice, not hers—Tasha still cared about her sister. She was all the family she had.

'You seem all right,' she said drily.

'All right?' Natalya squawked. 'Look at that. I'll be scarred. I just know I will!' she exclaimed, pointing to a tiny cut on her left cheek which had been cleaned and clearly didn't require stitches.

With the ease of long practice, Tasha ignored her sister's exclamation and sought information. 'What happened? All the patrolman said was that there had been an accident.' She recalled that moment of sick dread when she'd thought that she might have lost her only family. Orphaned since they were babies, there had only ever been the two of them—which was why Tasha still clung to the last threads of their relationship.

Blatantly ignoring the no-smoking sign, Natalya lit a cigarette and puffed away for several seconds before answering. 'God, it was awful. I thought I was going to die. A car went out of control as we were leaving the restaurant. It mounted the sidewalk and headed straight for us. Chase pushed me out of the way, but the car caught him. I hit the wall and got this!' Once again she indicated the tiny graze.

Tasha told herself not to be annoyed by her sister's self-absorption. If she wanted to know more she had to play it canny. 'Chase?'

Natalya blew out smoke and studied it intently. 'Chase Calder.'

Tasha caught her breath sharply. 'Chase Calder, the lawyer?' she said disbelievingly and, when her sister nodded, Tasha's eyes widened. She had heard of him. Who in the legal profession hadn't? His reputation as a trial lawyer was second to none. The man was a living legend at the age of thirty-four. 'How on earth did you meet him?'

'He came into the health club I use one day. We got talking. He was on a case, but it's finished now. I suppose you might as well know. We got engaged tonight,' she informed her sister casually.

Engaged? To say that Tasha was stunned was an understatement. She hadn't even known that Chase Calder was in Denver, and now she discovered that he was engaged to her sister. Engaged. She had never thought it would happen. She was so used to Natalya using men that it hadn't occurred to her that she might actually fall in love with one. Yet clearly she had. That it should be Chase Calder who had brought about the miracle was something of a surprise, but strange things did happen.

She stared at her sister, trying to imagine the anxiety Natalya was going through. It must be awful. That put a different complexion on her behaviour. Stress made people act in different ways. Her sister was clearly hiding hers behind a show of indifference.

Tasha's heart softened. 'How is he?' she asked gently.

Her sister stubbed out her cigarette and picked up her coat. 'Come and see for yourself.'

She led the way next door to where Chase Calder lay in a hospital bed, almost hidden behind the array of monitors to which he was hitched up. All Tasha could see was that he had dark hair and was dreadfully pale. It occurred to her that she had never actually seen a picture of him, and had no idea what he looked like.

'Have his relatives been notified?' Tasha asked in concern. If this man had been her son or brother then she would have wanted to know if he had been injured in an accident.

'Lord, don't ask me. I've got other things on my mind. They've just brought him back from the operating-room.' Natalya shuddered. 'It's touch and go whether he lives and, even if he does, chances are he's going to be a cripple!'

Dismayed, Tasha took her sister's hand. 'I'm so sorry,' she said, feeling totally inadequate.

Natalya shook her off. 'Don't be. I won't be around to see it!'

Tasha froze, and all notion of her sister suffering vanished. Nobody in love would be so downright callous. 'What do you mean?'

'Can you believe such rotten luck? I finally hook myself a man with both looks and money, and then he goes and half kills himself!' her sister declared with a bitter laugh.

That laugh was so out of place in this room, where a man lay seriously ill, that Tasha could only stare at her sibling in disbelief. 'I thought you loved him?'

'Love? Come on, Tasha, love is for the birds. I want money and position, and a man who can take me all the places I want to go. I'm damned if I'm going to be tied to a cripple!'

Disgust brought a wave of anger which Tasha had to swallow back before she could speak. 'He saved your life. You can't walk out on him now.'

Her sister raised one perfect eyebrow. 'Can't I? Just watch me.'

'He needs you, Nat,' Tasha stated, coldly furious.

'Well, I don't need him,' Natalya retorted, pulling a glittering engagement ring from her finger and tossing it down on the bed. 'Boy, what a waste of time!'

Tasha could hardly credit that they were related, so diametrically opposed were their views on life. 'You're unbelievable! I've made excuses for you over the years, Nat, but there's no excusing this.'

Her sister closed the gap between them and poked a finger in Tasha's chest. 'Listen, Miss Goody Two-Shoes, I don't care if you excuse me or not. But, if you're so concerned, why don't you stay with him? You're so frozen inside it wouldn't matter to you whether he could satisfy you or not! As for me, I'm out of here. There are plenty more fish in the sea. I think I'll try LA for a change.'

Tasha watched her twin walk out of the door without a backward glance, and felt ashamed. Even in her worst moments, she would never have thought that Natalya could act like that. She knew that *she* couldn't have done it. What Natalya had done was wrong from any standpoint.

Tasha turned away, her gaze falling on the stricken man. She walked closer to the bed, staring down at the still form—and found that she could not look away. Her lips parted on a tiny indrawn breath. He looked so vulnerable, lying there, with his handsome face a mass of scratches and bruises. At the sight of his helplessness something clutched at her heart and her throat closed over, making it incredibly difficult to swallow.

Her reaction surprised her, and she found herself having to rationalise it. I'm just suffering from reaction, she told herself. I'm grateful to him, even if Nat isn't, and so sorry that he had to be hurt like this. It was curiosity which kept her gaze on him.

So this was Chase Calder. Even unconscious, there was power in his face—a sense of purpose that gave character, so that although he was handsome there was nothing soft or weak in that. She wondered what colour eyes he had. All she could see were the longest lashes she had ever seen on a man, and his mouth had a sensuality which hinted at hidden fires. Fires which might never warm anyone again.

Why that thought should hurt her she couldn't imagine, but neither could she ignore the fact that it did. She felt as if someone had punched her in the chest, and it made the strength go out of her legs. Shaken, Tasha looked around for a chair but her eye was caught by the flash of light from the ring, which still lay on the covers. She picked it up, catching her breath at the beauty of the Ceylon sapphire with its circle of diamonds. It must have cost a small fortune, and her sister had tossed it away as if it were nothing! Just as she had tossed Chase Calder away.

Damn you, Nat, for seeing only dross where I see gold!

Looking around for her purse, Tasha belatedly remembered rushing out without it. She had simply stuffed keys and money into the pocket of her raincoat and dashed out. Grimacing, she knew that the only alternative to leaving the ring in her pocket, which was unthinkable, was to wear it. Then—wouldn't you know it—the only finger it fitted without being too loose or too tight was her marriage finger, and it gave her the strangest feeling to see it there. If she had been the fanciful type she might have read something into that, but Tasha prided herself on her level-headedness and knew that it was just coincidence.

A nurse came in, and Tasha stepped back to let her go about her business. She discovered as she stood by that she hated feeling helpless, unable to do anything save watch and wait. She couldn't recall ever feeling this anxious before. Of course, it was natural, considering that the man had saved her sister at considerable risk to himself. It was important that he be all right.

Unable to stand still, Tasha removed her raincoat and draped it over a chair to dry. Dragging her fingers through her hair, she tried to comb out the rat's tails. At least her suit, the black one she had worn in court with her white silk blouse, was dry. Smoothing it, she paced up and down until the nurse was free.

'Can you tell me if Mr Calder's family have been notified?'

The young nurse nodded. 'Oh, yes. I did it myself. They should be on their way by now.'

At least that was one less thing for her to worry about. 'Is there someone I can talk to about Mr Calder? I need to know if he's going to be all right.'

The nurse smiled with ready understanding. 'Sure. I'll have a word with Dr Cooper.'

Tasha nodded her thanks, and spent the next fifteen minutes pacing the floor and waiting for the doctor. She hadn't felt this nervous since waiting for the jury to come back in her first case. When the middle-aged woman in a white coat appeared Tasha made herself take a steadying breath.

Dr Cooper shook hands briefly. 'You'll be pleased to know Mr Calder is stable. The injuries he sustained were pretty severe, as we told you. The good thing is that his spine isn't damaged, which was what we feared at first.'

'So he will be able to walk?'

'Certainly.'

Tasha felt almost light-headed with relief. 'Thank God!'

'And the surgeon,' Dr Cooper added with a wry smile. 'How long he will have to remain in hospital we can't say. Mr Calder appears to be a very fit man, so that should help. And it's impossible to quantify the good it will do him to know you are here.'

That comment gave Tasha a jolt. She realised that the doctor thought she was Chase Calder's fiancée. About to put the matter straight, she abruptly closed her mouth. Explaining to Chase would be bad enough, and she could see no reason for hanging out her family's dirty linen for all to see. Besides, he deserved to know first because there would be nothing worse than hearing it through the grapevine. The sensible thing to do was to go along with the mistake for now.

'I won't be going anywhere, so long as he needs me,' Tasha promised. She had planned to stay because if there was anything she could do to speed his recovery she would do it. Someone had to make amends. He deserved better than to be abandoned. His brand of selflessness wasn't something you came by every day, and Natalya should have realised it.

Dr Cooper looked over at the still figure. 'He won't wake properly for several hours yet. Why don't you go home and get some rest?'

Tasha followed her gaze and shook her head. She was tired, but she had no intention of leaving just yet. 'His parents are flying out. I'll wait for them,' she insisted, and the doctor knew from experience when it was futile to pursue the matter.

Alone again, Tasha drew another chair up to the bed and sat down. One tanned hand rested on top of the covers, long-fingered and capable. Without thinking, she reached out and touched it. His flesh was warm, and it was the most natural thing in the world to curl her fingers around his. She sought to give comfort and, instead, found herself receiving it. Amazingly, the tension went out of her and she sighed, making herself more comfortable.

Silence settled around them, except for the steady beeping of the monitors. Tiredness began to overtake her. She had had a busy day at work and a battle in court, followed by the shock of the accident. The nervous energy which had kept her going began to seep out, and she felt weary to her bones. Little by little her eyes slowly closed.

'Nat-Natasha?'

The pained voice drew Tasha from sleep. She felt disorientated and blinked and looked around, unfocused for a second before memory returned. She had no idea what time it was, only that she was at the hospital and Chase Calder was awake.

'Natasha?' The voice was more urgent this time.

Tasha rose from the chair with the knowledge that

Natalya had been calling herself Natasha again. There was nothing wrong in that, she supposed. Her twin had always preferred it to her given name. Now that they weren't together any more she must be using it all the time.

Bending over the bed—intent on reassuring him—Tasha looked down into a pair of the most astonishing silvery grey eyes and, without warning, tumbled into their fathomless depths. Her lips parted on a sharply indrawn breath as her stomach lurched and her heart kicked into a frantic beat. Something seemed to shift on its axis inside her. Her brain shut down, but on a purely sensory level she went into overdrive. It was as if every nerve in her body had come alive. Switched on by an electric pulse which throbbed through her.

'Natasha?'

For a third time he said her name, but this time with concern. As if she were coming out of a drugged sleep, she stared down at him dizzily—her mouth dry, her heart thumping. Unnerved by what had just happened, she struggled for composure—helped by the pain she saw, clouding his eyes.

'I'm here,' she answered thickly, squeezing his hand comfortingly.

Chase Calder swallowed painfully, and his breathing was dreadfully shallow. 'Are you…OK?'

No, she wasn't. She didn't know if she ever would be again, but that wasn't what he'd meant. He wanted to know that the woman he loved had sustained no injuries. There would be time enough later to tell him that she wasn't who he thought she was. That Natalya wasn't what he thought, either. For now, he needed to be reassured. 'I'm fine. Try not to talk, Chase. You've been hurt.'

He tried to lift his head, and groaned with sudden pain. 'How bad?'

With her free hand she began to comb her fingers through his damp hair. Lord, it felt so silky, and as it curled around her fingers she felt identical tendrils tightening about her heart. It was the craziest sensation and, because she didn't know how to deal with it, she did her best to ignore it.

'They've had to operate on you. I don't know all the details, but they said you're going to be OK.' She saw his eyes flicker shut and she sighed, reluctantly moving away.

His fingers tightened so fiercely around hers that she had to bite her lip to not cry out. He was looking at her through narrow slits. 'Stay with me,' he gritted out, fighting to keep his eyes open. It was a battle he lost almost at once, and Tasha knew that that brief moment of waking was over. He was unconscious again.

'I will,' she promised, feeling his fingers slacken and fall away. 'I'll be right beside you,' she added, even though he couldn't hear her.

As the silence settled around her once more Tasha was left to face the result of these last few incredible minutes. It made her feel shaky, just thinking about it. What had happened? One minute she had been intent only on reassurance, and the next... It had been the most incredible sensation. She'd never experienced anything like it. She had looked into Chase Calder's eyes, and he had seemed to fill every part of her. Every one of her dormant senses had recognised him. It had been astounding. Earthshattering. But what was it?

She looked at him again and, as if compelled, she raised a hand and ran it softly and questioningly over his cheek. Then it hit her, sending her all of a tremble.

No! It couldn't be! She couldn't possibly be falling in love with him...could she?

As if scalded, she jerked her hand away. No! Definitely not. She was a level-headed, unemotional person, and that sort of thing just didn't happen! So what was it? the tiny voice in her head demanded mockingly. Tasha didn't know but there had to be a perfectly good explanation why, after one look into those incredible eyes, she had felt as if she had known him for ever. He was absolutely, most definitely, not the missing piece which made her complete! she decided firmly.

Her breath left her throat in a shaky sigh, and she raised a hand and dragged it through her hair. She had to get a grip on herself. It had been a traumatic day, and she was simply overreacting. A good night's sleep would do wonders for her perspective.

Comforted by that sensible piece of advice, Tasha walked away from the bed and took up a position by the window—staring out into the darkness.

She wasn't sure how much time had passed when the sound of footsteps made her turn around. Two people entered the room, looking travel-weary—their faces pale and drawn with concern. The couple were somewhere in their sixties, and the likeness of the man to the younger man in the bed would have told Tasha who they were even if she hadn't expected them.

'You're Chase's parents,' she greeted them, smiling warmly as she walked towards them.

The woman, a little younger than the man, smiled back tensely. 'I'm Elaine Calder, and this is my husband, John. You must be Natasha. Chase told us all about you. It's dreadful that we have to meet this way.' Her words choked off as she stared across at her unmoving son. Tears filled her eyes, drawing Tasha's compassion.

'Please don't get upset. I know it looks awful, but they

say he's doing all right,' Tasha hastened to reassure her, knowing that that was more important right this second than clearing up the error over her name. 'Perhaps you would rather speak to a doctor?'

'In a moment,' John Calder demurred, halting her move towards the door. He had to clear a throat tight with emotion to continue. 'The nurse who rang us said our son was hurt in an accident. Were you there?'

Again Tasha was confronted with an unenviable choice. She did not particularly want to protect her sister's reputation, but neither did she think it was fair to tell anyone what Natalya had done until Chase knew. Not even his parents. He had the painful right to be told first, and she would not shirk from telling the truth. When he was well enough to hear it. It would be his choice then as to whom he told, and what. Until then she would cover up for Natalya. Something her sister would not thank her for but, then, she wouldn't know.

'Yes. He was protecting me,' she declared, and quickly told them the few facts that Natalya had told her.

'Oh, my goodness! Are you all right?' Elaine Calder was instantly all concern, and Tasha felt colour steal into her cheeks. Damn Nat for putting them all through this fiasco!

'I'm fine. Not a scratch,' she replied uncomfortably. She never had liked lying. Natalya, now, was gold-medal standard!

'Thank the Lord! It must have been quite a shock, though, Natasha,' Mrs Calder said solicitously.

'Tasha, please. Natasha is shortened to Tasha,' she invited, hoping to divert them from asking things to which she didn't know the answer.

Elaine Calder smiled at her. 'Tasha sounds lovely,

dear. I'm so thankful you were unhurt. Chase would have been devastated to lose you.'

That was what worried Tasha so much. Chase's re-action to the news. He'd been hurt enough already, and she hated to give him more pain. The only way she could think of to soften the blow was to make sure that he was well and truly fit enough to take the truth. If he loved Natalya the way she believed he must then, whenever he heard it, it would be devastating.

She was amazed how it hurt her to think of inflicting pain on him. In that moment she really began to hate her twin. Chase Calder's love had been used and re-jected. She would never forgive Natalya for deserting him when he needed her most.

Burning with a fiercely protective rage, Tasha turned to the other woman. 'Mrs Calder, I want you to know that I would never willingly hurt your son,' she declared passionately.

Elaine Calder closed the space between them and took Tasha's hand in hers. 'I know that, dear.'

Tasha sighed, surprised by the depth of her own emo-tions. It was probably years of suppressed anger which had suddenly come to a head. 'Why don't you go and see Chase for yourself while I go and find Dr Cooper?' she suggested, and the Calders were only too ready to fall in with her plan.

Dr Cooper took Chase's parents back to her office to fill them in on all that had been done. Tasha stayed with Chase until they returned and then, at their suggestion, took herself off home. She told herself that it was as-sociated guilt that made her so reluctant to go.

Back at her apartment half an hour later Tasha barely had the energy to shower and change into a nightdress, before collapsing onto her bed—totally exhausted. As sleep claimed her her thoughts were full of a man with silvery grey eyes. When he had looked at her those eyes had seemed to pierce right through to her soul. Now they haunted her dreams, filling her with a profound sense of loss.

It was bright sunshine when Tasha awoke the next morning, feeling rested but at the same time strangely restless. She had vague memories of her dreams but, then, it would have been surprising if she hadn't dreamt about Chase Calder after all that had happened.

Showering and dressing in another of the white silk blouse and tailored suits she favoured for work, Tasha made herself a breakfast of toast and coffee then rang the office. She worked for a large law company, where she was still very much a junior. Her friend Annie worked in Reception, and promised to pass on the message that Tasha would be late. Fortunately she wasn't due in court again for another week or so, and any appointments could easily be rescheduled.

That done, she collected her purse and briefcase and was half out of the door before she remembered the engagement ring, lying on her bedside table. Running back for it, she was about to put it in her purse when she realised that as everyone at the hospital believed that she was Chase Calder's fiancée they would find it odd if she didn't wear his ring. She felt uncomfortable wearing it, though, and would be glad when she could finally return it. Satisfied that she had forgotten nothing else, she hurried out to catch a bus.

Ordinarily she would have used her car, but it was just her luck that at the moment it was being serviced. That meant relying on public transport until she got it back, which would hopefully not be too long now.

Traffic was its usual snarl-up, and she was later than she'd hoped when she took the elevator up to Chase's floor. It gave her nerves a terrible shock to see Elaine Calder pacing about outside his room when she approached it. As soon as the other woman saw her she virtually pounced on her.

'Tasha, thank goodness! I tried to phone you, but you must have just left.'

Tasha's heart dropped like lead. 'What is it? What's happened?' Alarm shot through her system like wildfire. Dear God, no! He couldn't be dead! The possibility froze the blood in her veins, leaving her feeling more stricken than she could ever have thought possible.

Elaine took a calming breath. 'Come with me, dear. Before you see Chase Dr Cooper needs to talk to you,' she said worriedly, and Tasha suddenly discovered that she couldn't move.

'He's dead, isn't he?' she said flatly, feeling her heart crack wide open.

The older woman's eyes became round with horror when she realised what Tasha thought. 'No! Oh, Tasha, dear, I'm so sorry. I never meant for you to think that!' she exclaimed remorsefully.

Tasha had to close her eyes for a moment to fight off a wave of dizziness. Dear God, she had thought…she had thought… She paled. Why had the thought been so devastating? She hardly knew the man! It was ridiculous, getting this emotional over a stranger! Anyone would think…

She brought her thoughts back under tight control at that wayward piece of imagining. It wasn't true. She was not in love with Chase Calder! She was just…just feeling responsible. That was all.

Hoping that she didn't still look as pale on the outside as she felt inside, Tasha looked at Chase's mother for confirmation. 'He's all right?' Seeing Elaine's nod, she managed to smile. 'I guess I overreacted.'

Elaine patted her hand and drew her away from Chase's room to a door further down the corridor. 'We do tend to overreact when the person we love is hurt,' she said, smiling confidentially. Tasha winced inwardly, reminding herself that just because everyone believed that she was in love that didn't mean she was.

Dr Cooper was seated behind a cluttered desk, and she waved them into the chairs opposite. Only when they were seated did she lean forward across the desk, her hands firmly clasped as she studied Tasha.

'Thank you for coming to see me, Miss Larsen. Something happened earlier, of which I feel you should be appraised. Mr Calder returned to consciousness about thirty minutes ago, and asked for you. He got very agitated when his parents explained that you weren't here. So much so that we had to medicate him. Apparently, he thought they were hiding the fact that you were dead.'

Tasha uttered a tiny gasp. 'But I spoke to him last night!'

Dr Cooper shrugged. 'Clearly he doesn't remember the incident. That's not unusual. However, I'm sure you can understand that agitation of any sort is not going to help his recovery, and might seriously hinder it.'

'I understand,' Tasha nodded. 'How can I help?'

'It's really very simple. Your fiancé is asleep right now, but he will have longer periods of consciousness. All I'm asking is that you be there with him when he does wake up to convince him that you really are alive. The more often he sees you the more he will relax. Can you do that?'

Having considered the worst of possibilities just moments ago, this request was a snip. She would do it, and gladly. 'Of course. Fortunately, I'm not due in court today or that might have been a problem. I'll phone the office and take the day off,' she said without hesitation.

'You're a lawyer?' Elaine Calder exclaimed, and Tasha smiled wryly.

'Yes, but not in Chase's league,' she admitted, and saw the other woman frown for a moment.

'I wonder why he didn't say? Still, it's not important. Getting him well again is our priority, isn't it, dear?' She beamed at Tasha who nodded back, only then becoming aware of the fact that she had no idea what Natalya had told Chase about herself. Still, she couldn't worry about what she didn't know. She would just have to hope that she could field whatever came her way.

A bleeper went off just then, and Dr Cooper took it from her pocket and reached for the phone. 'Excuse me.'

They left her to her call and made their way back to Chase's room.

'I rang Evan and Alison last night to tell them Chase was going to be OK,' Elaine said conversationally, slipping her arm through Tasha's.

'Evan and Alison?' Tasha parroted, not having a clue who they were.

The other woman looked at her in surprise. 'Chase's brother and sister. He must have told you about them.'

Tasha winced inwardly. Of course Chase would have told his fiancée, which was why she didn't know anything about them. 'Oh, yes,' she confirmed, laughing at her own stupidity. 'My mind is just nowhere this morning,' she apologised.

'That's all right, dear. I quite understand. You've been through a lot. Besides, you've not known Chase very long. You might say it was a whirlwind romance!' Elaine said with a chuckle.

Mrs Calder had no idea just how much of an understatement that was, Tasha thought. I don't even know when we were supposed to have met! I'm walking blindfold through a room full of pitfalls!

'Were you surprised it was so quick?' she asked, knowing that at least was a safe question.

Elaine pulled a wry face. 'Just a bit. After all, Chase had only come out here less than a month ago to take a case as a favour to his father. John used to be head of the family law firm until he retired last year. The client is an old friend of the family. Anyway, as I was saying, when Chase rang us not long after he arrived to say that he had met the woman he planned to marry I was a little surprised. I admit I was worried but, having met you, I have no more doubts,' Elaine finished warmly.

Tasha groaned silently. This was getting entirely too complicated, but she could see no way out for the moment. She forced herself to concentrate on what she had just learned. Chase had known Natalya less than a month. Elaine was right. It had been a whirlwind romance, but whereas Chase had clearly fallen in love the same could not be said for her sister. Chase must have believed that he had found happiness but, instead—as he had yet to discover—he had found only pain.

CHAPTER TWO

TASHA stood by the window of Chase's room and stared out at the ant-like movements of the people down below. It had been hours since she had phoned her office and arranged to take the whole day off. Chase had stirred several times, but hadn't woken up yet. Half an hour ago Tasha had finally persuaded the Calders to take time away from their constant vigil and get some rest and a decent meal. They would be no use to their son with their nerves worn to a frazzle.

'Natasha?'

His voice was barely above a croaked whisper, yet Tasha heard it and she closed her eyes. She had been expecting this moment with a kind of dreadful foreboding. Her reaction earlier had more than somewhat unnerved her. So much so that she was actually fearful of approaching the bed and the man who occupied it. Yet she had promised to help and so, squaring her shoulders, she turned her back on the view and crossed to the bed.

'I'm here,' she said calmly, while her heart went up a gear.

He was watching her with those stunning grey eyes. Sweet heaven, what they did to her! They made her heart turn over and her knees go weak. It would be so very easy to drown in them, never caring if she ever surfaced again. It was a thought which set her blood whizzing through her veins and produced a wave of heat that made her skin bloom.

This can't be happening, she told herself helplessly. I'm a woman who prides herself on logic. How can I suddenly become this mess of emotions? She had no answer she was prepared to accept.

As she stopped by the bed Chase held out his hand, and she was compelled to take it. Something akin to an electric charge shot up her arm, making her catch her breath. Her eyes turned into turbulent blue pools into which Chase stared with an equal amount of surprise. The knowledge that he must have felt it too made her shiver, but not with anything resembling distaste. On the contrary.

Chase blinked at her in bemusement. 'It's amazing what…a brush with death…can do,' he murmured, breathing carefully because of his damaged ribs.

Tasha became more confused. 'What?'

He took a deep breath, wincing at the pain it caused him. 'Touching you told me…I'm not dead yet,' he told her sardonically, and as she followed the direction of his eyes down the bed she realised what he meant and hot colour surged into her cheeks.

Tasha immediately wanted to step back out of range of his mesmerising influence but he wouldn't let her hand go and, fearful of hurting him, she was forced to subside. 'Maybe I should get them to put something in your tea!' she rebuked him, and he uttered a laugh which ended on a groan. 'Chase?' she queried in swift alarm, and he shook his head.

'I'm OK,' he confirmed, and after a moment or two he looked at her accusingly. 'It's your fault… You started it.'

'My fault?' Tasha yelped, wishing that he would let her hand go. She might be able to think then. She needed room. He was too close.

'You shouldn't have…looked at me as…if you wanted to…eat me!' he told her shockingly, and her chin dropped.

'I did not!' she protested faintly.

'You did, but...don't worry...I liked it.'

Deeply embarrassed, Tasha wished that the floor would open up because she was afraid that what he'd said was true. The floor remained solid, leaving her only denial. 'This is absurd. I...I came here to help you get better!'

'It worked.'

Tasha bit her lip and looked away. God, she couldn't cope with this. The way he was making her feel so jumbled up inside. This was not the way she had expected to talk to a man who had so nearly died. She wasn't handling it at all well. She cleared her throat nervously. 'Will you please behave?'

'I can't do much else...can I?' he informed her ironically, and she rolled her eyes.

'What can I do with you?' she exclaimed in exasperation, glaring at him.

'I have some...suggestions, but I...don't think I'm up to it,' he responded and, in spite of herself, Tasha laughed.

'You're incorrigible!'

'That's...encouraging.'

She sighed as she studied his face, seeing beyond the attempts at humour to the pain beneath. Her heart twisted anxiously. 'How do you feel?'

A flash of a smile tweaked at his lips. 'Like I've been...hit by a car!'

Tasha caught her breath. How could he joke about it? 'What were you trying to do? Prove you were as invincible out of court as you are in it?' she charged, then could have died when she realised what she had said. Dear God, how could she have said that when the man had been saving her life, as he believed?

Far from being aggrieved, the glint in his eye was

appreciative. 'The jury's still out…on that one,' he replied, and a wave of colour stormed into her cheeks.

'I'm sorry, I shouldn't have said that.'

'No problem… I rather like it…when you get mad at me,' he teased, making her heart flutter in her chest.

Heavens, but the man could charm the birds out of the trees. 'It was ungrateful.'

'So, when I'm better, I'll…let you apologise properly… How's that?'

Tasha met his dancing eyes and groaned inwardly. He was too much. He turned her inside out, and made her begin to think that she didn't even care! What was the matter with her? She just had to get a grip on herself.

Striving for her best courtroom manner, she gave him a cool look. 'I'll think about it.'

'So will I,' Chase promised with a warmth that shivered up her spine.

'God, you make me want to hit you!' Tasha exploded, pulling free this time because his hold had slackened. She walked to the end of the bed and stood there, breathing heavily. To her disbelief, she actually heard him chuckle.

'You wouldn't hit a…sick man, would you?'

She spun round, opened her mouth to say something sharp then closed it again. Crossing her arms, she eyed him threateningly. 'Don't tempt me!'

The look that came into his eyes then seemed to steal all the air from the room. 'It's good to know I can,' he breathed huskily, and Tasha felt the muscles in her stomach clench.

'Chase Calder, so help me, I'll…' She tailed off with a sound of frustration. Finally she turned confused blue eyes on him. 'What are you doing to me?'

'Only what you're…doing to me.'

That didn't help. She paced up and down. 'I used to

be a sane and sensible person till you came into my life!'
And, if she wanted to retain that sanity, she would have
to get out of his life as soon as possible.

'Ditto,' he murmured, making her nerves jolt and
drawing her gaze to the bed, where she was in time to
see him wince. She forgot all about her own troubles
instantly. 'What happened? Are you in pain?' she asked
in instant concern.

'Dry,' he croaked. 'Mouth feels like...a desert.'

'I'd better ring for a nurse. I'm not sure what you
should have.' She reached for the buzzer and pressed it.

'Tell me... My parents...were they here?' Chase
asked, no longer smiling or teasing, and, with compunc-
tion, Tasha realised that he was exhausted.

Automatically her free hand brushed his hair off his
forehead, but somehow she forgot to stop combing her
fingers through it as she studied him. 'They were, but
they've gone to get something to eat. They'll be back
soon.'

The nurse arrived then, and by the time she had finished making him more comfortable Chase was getting
drowsy again. Not very long after that he fell asleep.

Tasha sank onto a nearby chair, staring at his profile.
Those absurdly long lashes, resting on his cheek, made
him look so boyish and vulnerable. While he slept the
power he had over her was dimmed, and she could think
again. Those thoughts were not happy.

She had meant to reassure him and, instead, they had
ended up having a conversation alive with innuendo.
Which, heaven help her, she had actually enjoyed! That,
together with the way he affected her, was a lethal com-
bination and told her one thing. Last night had not been
a product of stress. One look at him and she had turned
to mush inside—a victim of her rioting emotions.

Her nerves fluttered, and she swallowed a lump which

had settled in her throat. She knew what was happening. She wasn't that naïve. She was caught in the grip of a powerful attraction, and she knew why. Last night she had refused to consider it, but after today she couldn't deny it. She had fallen in love with Chase Calder. It was the only explanation that fitted. She'd heard about people falling in love at first sight, but had discounted it as unlikely. Now she knew that it wasn't because it had happened to her. She had only to look into his eyes and she was lost.

Lost in the eyes of a man who thought she was another woman!

That was a choker, and it made her blood chill. It was like walking into a nightmare. How could she have been foolish enough to fall in love with her sister's fiancé? Because she couldn't help it. She had been fathoms deep before she'd ever known what was happening. But she knew now, and she couldn't allow it to continue. It should be easy. All she had to do was keep reminding herself that he didn't want *her*. He was responding to the woman he believed her to be. That should cool the fire in her blood more quickly than anything!

All she had to do was keep her head, and her distance, and in a few days tell him about Natalya. That revelation should put the lid on this unfortunate attraction.

Fighting a sense of dejection, she picked up a magazine Elaine Calder had left behind and flipped open the pages randomly—forcing her mind to concentrate on the words before her and not the man in the bed.

When the Calders returned, several hours later, Tasha gave them a brief account of what had happened.

'He hasn't stirred since? Then his mind must be at ease at last,' his mother declared in relief, and Tasha smiled. She liked the Calders, and truly regretted that she wasn't telling them the truth. She only hoped that they would understand her reasons later.

John Calder smiled at her, reminding her even more of Chase. 'A few more days of looking at that lovely face of yours and he'll forget he was ever in an accident,' he teased her, and Tasha realised where Chase got his charm.

'Unfortunately, looks can be more of a hindrance than a help,' she remarked drily, and he nodded understandingly.

'Elaine told me you were a lawyer. No doubt you've come up against sexism many times. Too many men find beauty and brains intimidating, and have to put it down,' he commented seriously, and Tasha grimaced.

'But not you,' she declared with certainty.

John Calder acknowledged that truth with an inclination of his head. 'Not me. I have too much respect for the sharpness of the female intellect. So, I might add, does my son.' A statement she had no reason to question.

'If he is anything like you, Mr Calder, then I would not doubt it,' she said smoothly, beginning to gather her things together, and both Calders laughed.

'He's susceptible to flattery, too, just like Chase,' Elaine teased, helping Tasha on with her coat. 'Thank you for today, dear. Will we see you tonight?'

They were treating her like one of the family, and Tasha felt her conscience stir uncomfortably. Yet there was nothing she could do, except accept it gracefully. 'I'll pop in later, but there's something I have to do first,' she compromised, and gave in to the urge to drop a kiss on the older woman's cheek before she left the room.

The business she had to take care of was not something she looked forward to. Though she was loath, she had to go and visit her sister and try one last time to get her to change her mind. She didn't particularly want

Natalya to get back with Chase because she wanted to protect him from the kind of hurt her sister had inflicted. However, that was not her choice. If Chase wanted her sister, then her conscience wouldn't let her go on without another try.

She took a cab to the block of stylish apartments where Natalya lived. The security guard was one of the few people who knew that she and Natalya were twins, and he identified her by the length of her hair. She expected to be waved through the lobby but, instead, he called her to the desk.

'Sorry, Miss Larsen, your sister's not here.'

Which didn't really surprise Tasha at all. 'Do you know when she'll be back?' She could leave a message, asking Natalya to call her.

'No, ma'am. I mean she's not here. She's gone.'

Tasha blinked at him foolishly. 'Gone?'

The guard looked uncomfortable. 'Packed up her things, paid her rent and left town first thing this morning. Sorry, ma'am.'

Stunned by the swiftness of Natalya's departure, Tasha shook her head. 'That's OK. It's not your fault she didn't tell me. Did she happen to say where she was going?'

'The coast, was all she said.' He shrugged apologetically. 'Shall I call you a cab?'

'Thanks. I'll wait for it outside.'

Well, Tasha thought as she sat on a low brick wall to wait, that was quick. She really hadn't thought that her sister would act quite so fast. Nor leave, without saying goodbye. But, then, Natalya had always been a law unto herself. The woman who could abandon a seriously injured man could do just about anything. Still, it told her what she needed to know.

Natalya wanted nothing to do with Chase. It shouldn't

have made her feel so pleased, but there was no denying that it did. Tasha had done all that her conscience had told her to do, regarding her sister. What happened next was up to her. Her actions certainly wouldn't break her sister's heart because Natalya didn't have one!

By Friday afternoon Tasha was convinced that she had her wayward emotions under control. She had visited Chase several times every day—having her car back had been a godsend—and there had been no repeat of that mind-blowing attraction. Oh, she was very much aware of him. Even injured, Chase Calder was not the sort of man who could be ignored but she had a handle on it.

Possibly because her visits had mostly coincided with times when Chase was asleep or other people were present, she conceded wryly. Nevertheless, she was sure that she had her senses under control. Work had helped. It had been easy to bury herself in research and the legal technicalities of her workload. Which had, in its turn, reinforced her conviction. If she was really in love her mind would be all over the place. It wasn't, and on that she rested her case.

Today she had left the office a little earlier to allow John and Elaine to do some necessary shopping, and had brought flowers with her to brighten up the sterile look of the room. Most of the monitors had been switched off now, and Dr Cooper had told them that Chase would be moved into a private room tomorrow.

She was humming to herself, while arranging the flowers in a vase, when Chase spoke.

'What have you done to your hair?'

Having believed him to be still asleep, Tasha jumped sharply. 'You scared the life out of me!' she declared, pressing a hand to her thundering heart as she glanced round.

'Sorry,' Chase apologised unrepentantly, showing her for the first time his attractively quirky grin which sent a flash fire through her nerves before she could stop it.

Tasha's eyes became glued to the dimple which had appeared beside his mouth. The sight of it made her heart do a funny kind of flip-flop in her chest. Oh, God, she groaned silently. She had been prepared for his eyes and had been determined not to look into them, but he had blind-sided her with that smile.

Her conviction withered and died as she realised that his attraction for her seemed endless. Even as she watched the dimple disappeared, and she lifted her head a fraction. She met his eyes and caught her breath at the heat she saw there. It raised her own temperature considerably.

Her smile came and went and she moistened her lips nervously, an action he followed with such interest that her stomach clenched. The room suddenly seemed to be crackling with electricity and she dragged in a breath, telling herself to say something before she shattered from the swift rise in tension.

'I was miles away,' she explained scratchily. 'I tend to hum when I'm concentrating on something.'

'I noticed,' he drawled huskily, breathing carefully to minimise the pain of his ribs. For a moment they gazed into each other's eyes in silence and, to Tasha, it felt as if something elemental shimmered in the air between them, stealing what little breath she had left. 'So?' he prompted with another smile.

For the life of her Tasha had no idea what he was talking about. 'So?' she croaked back.

Chase lifted a hand and pointed, wincing at the effort it took to do even that much. 'Your hair.'

Her hair? In confusion she raised a hand to it and then realised what he meant, and her eyes widened. She had completely forgotten that Natalya always wore her hair long. 'Oh, I…er… It was getting on my nerves, so I had it cut.' Lord, she sounded like an utter fool, but Chase had the ability to drive every sane thought from her mind.

'Pity. I dreamed of burying my face in it when we made love,' he told her shockingly, and colour stormed into her cheeks.

'Chase!' she gasped, but not in protest. It was pure reaction to the mental vision she had of his fantasy, which she found stunningly arousing.

'Say that again,' he ordered softly with a groan which had absolutely nothing to do with pain.

Dear God, he was making the hairs stand up on her flesh! It was as if every sense she possessed had come vitally alive. She'd never experienced anything like it in her life before meeting him. 'Say what?' she breathed, floundering under her own responses.

'My name. There's a sort of catch you put in it that's damned sexy,' Chase added with the sort of look that, had he been fit, would have made her melt on the spot. She very nearly did, anyway. Her legs felt as if they had no bones in them.

Tasha's mind ceased functioning on a sensible level at that point. All she knew was what she was feeling, and how Chase was reacting. 'Are you flirting with me?' she asked breathlessly.

The glitter in his eye became a flame. 'Don't you know?'

There was the width of the room between them, and yet she felt as if he'd touched her and she could hardly breathe! 'Do you… Do you think that's wise?'

He groaned tellingly. 'Probably not, but I had to make sure I hadn't lost my touch,' he responded wryly, and Tasha very nearly groaned with him.

'Believe me, you haven't,' she assured him tartly, making him laugh. Instantly she wished she hadn't because it had clearly hurt him. 'Are you OK?'

'I'd feel better if you were over here instead of over there,' he admitted, and held out his hand, and—like a moth to a flame—she came and took it. The second they touched that positive charge shivered through her, and her lashes fluttered down over darkening eyes.

'Amazing, isn't it?' he declared softly, linking their fingers and drawing her dark blue gaze.

'Do you…?' she began, then her throat closed over as he nodded.

'To the roots of my hair. I keep thinking of what I would have been missing if I'd died.'

Where moments ago her blood had been sizzling hot now it ran cold, chilling her to her soul. If he had died. The words made her shudder.

'Natasha? What's wrong?' The concern in Chase's voice brought her stricken gaze to his.

'You could have died,' she intoned flatly, only in that moment realising just what he meant to her and how she had come perilously close to losing him before she'd ever found him. She had had a vision of a world without him in it, and it had been bleak beyond description. The depth of her emotion staggered her. Two days ago he had just been a name, but now he was so much more that it frightened her.

Chase's fingers closed tightly about hers. 'Don't think about it, sweetheart. It didn't happen. I'm alive,' he declared forcefully.

Tasha stared at him, seeing the strength of the man he was—despite being in a hospital bed. Yes, he was very much alive and she had never been more thankful.

'I'm glad,' she said huskily, and because she knew that she couldn't take much more right now changed the subject. 'You haven't told me whether you like my hair this way.'

Distracted, he studied her for a moment then nodded. 'It suits you.'

Her smile blossomed quite naturally. 'Why, thank you. Tactful, but nice to hear anyway,' she laughed, recovering her poise. Later she would have to think about what she had discovered, but not now.

'We aim to please,' he intoned like an unctuous store clerk, and she laughed again. Oh, he did please. Very much so.

Her eyes fell to his jaw. 'I see you've decided to sport designer stubble. It makes you look incredibly...' She had been about to add 'sexy', and hastily cut herself off. But it was too late—one look at his eyes told her that he knew exactly what she had been going to say.

'A fine thing to say when I'm as weak as a kitten and unable to do anything about it!' Chase berated her, studying her pink cheeks with interest. 'You're not wearing any make-up.'

This time Tasha didn't bat an eyelid, although she had forgotten that Natalya wouldn't be seen dead without her 'face'.

'I decided I would look foolish swanning round the hospital like a film star,' she invented swiftly, trusting that he didn't know Natalya so well that he'd realise that was what she would like to do!

Apparently he didn't because he didn't debate the point. 'Seeing you like this, I wonder why you bother with make-up at all. You look beautiful without it. Those eyes!'

Tasha found herself holding her breath, mesmerised by the way he was looking at her. She knew all about eyes. Every time she looked into his she wanted to drown in them. Forget everything and just...

'Darling, you're awake!' Elaine Calder's cheery exclamation from across the room broke the spell, and Tasha took a quick step backwards as Chase's mother bustled over and bent to kiss him carefully. 'Ouch. You could do with a shave!'

'One of the nurses offered, but I'd rather have Dad do it.'

Tasha had diplomatically removed herself from the family and returned to the flowers she had been arranging, but she glanced round at that. 'Don't tell me you'd refuse if that pretty little blonde one offered. The one who bats her eyes at you every time she comes in here,' she taunted softly.

'Jealous?' he returned smartly, and she raised an eyebrow at him.

'Should I be?'

'Oh, you two!' Elaine sighed indulgently. 'Anyone with half a mind can see you're loopy about each other! The atmosphere is positively electric in here,' she observed drily. 'Now, if I can interrupt for just a second, can you tell me how you feel today?' Her motherly gaze was searching as it scanned Chase's face.

'Like I've been sparring with Tyson!' he responded with feeling and, although everyone laughed, Tasha could see the strain beginning to show on his face. She admired his spirit. He was going to need it in the days ahead. She couldn't begin to imagine the pain he was in, but that he felt it was clear from the white line around his mouth.

John Calder laid a hand on his son's shoulder. 'Just you stay in there fighting, son. And don't you worry. I'll bring a razor with me next time.'

'Thanks, Dad.'

'Has Tasha been taking good care of you while we

were gone?' Elaine queried as she straightened the bed-clothes unnecessarily.

Chase caught his mother's hand. 'Stop fussing, Mom! And that's another thing. Why do you keep calling her Tasha?' he snapped, made irritable by the increasing pain of his injuries.

His parents didn't exactly freeze, but they did look perplexed.

'Don't you?' Elaine asked in confusion, turning to look at Tasha.

What else could go wrong? How stupid of her to tell his parents her name and not tell Chase too. She could only put it down to shock, and the fact that just being in the same room with him addled her brain so that it was a wonder she thought at all!

Tasha picked up the vase and carried it over to the table beside his bed. 'Your parents call me Tasha because it's short for Natasha,' she said with remarkable sang-froid. She placed the vase down, and stepped back to admire it. Her heart thumped as she crossed her arms and transferred her open gaze to his frowning one.

'Why didn't you tell me before?' he challenged, sounding baffled—as well he might.

Why, indeed? She shrugged. 'I thought you preferred to call me Natasha,' she invented blithely, for what else could she say? She wasn't surprised when he stared at her blankly.

'I didn't know I had a choice,' Chase argued fairly, and she conceded that he had cause to be miffed.

As she glanced round their faces all she saw was a kind of bemusement. Tasha thought, Oh, hell, and lowered her head to smile into his eyes. 'Does it really matter, darling?' she asked throatily, and experienced a dart of pleasure when she saw him swallow.

Chase cleared his throat. 'I guess we still have a lot

to learn about each other. And, no, it doesn't matter. As a matter of fact, Tasha is more you with your hair cut short and no make-up. I think I prefer it.'

'I'm glad because I prefer it too,' she said unsteadily, and met the distracted look in his eyes for a moment, before straightening up.

Tasha bit her lip as she turned away, unwilling to let him see the colour in her cheeks. Colour brought about by the knowledge that she, Tasha Larsen, could disconcert a man such as Chase Calder.

She stayed until Chase finally drifted off to sleep again, exhausted by the effort required to keep up a conversation. On her way home she called into a shopping mall to stock up on some much-needed groceries. She felt light-hearted, buoyed up by her newly discovered power, so that what was usually a chore was actually quite fun until she was reaching for a jar of mayonnaise—and her bubble burst.

What on earth was she doing, flirting with Chase Calder? He responded to her because he thought she was Natalya! The elation she had felt such a short time ago vanished in the face of reality. She had fallen in love with her sister's fiancé and, because of that, there would be no future for her with him. Any day now she was going to have to tell him the truth and, when Chase discovered what Natalya had done, he would hate her. Tasha wouldn't blame him. And though he might not hate Natalya's twin, he would have no reason to love her.

She might love him, but he didn't love her. He was attracted, but that was something altogether different. The truth was like a douche of cold water, and she realised that she had been behaving like an idiot. She hadn't been using her brain, and now she had to retrieve the pieces of her shattered heart. It hurt, but she had her pride. She couldn't have given too much away so it should be easy to cover her tracks.

She couldn't hide her attraction, but she could make sure that he didn't guess it had ever gone deeper than that. It was time for damage limitation. For her own sake, she must do what she had told herself before—keep her head and keep her distance.

She finished her shopping with grim determination and drove home to her comfortable, if not so fashionably located, apartment. Leaving the bags on the kitchen counter, she was about to go and take a shower when her eye caught the light flashing on her answering machine. Automatically she detoured into the lounge to check it.

'Hi, it's Annie. Just checking that everything's OK for tonight. Bye.'

Tasha clapped a hand to her forehead. Stevie! She'd completely forgotten about him. He was the ten-year-old son of her co-worker and best friend, Annie, and she had promised to take him to the ball game tonight. She had bought the tickets ages ago, knowing that it was the boy's birthday tomorrow.

As a distraction, the reminder couldn't have come at a better time. She had planned to visit Chase tonight as usual, but this was her opportunity to begin putting her life back in order. Though part of her rebelled, the sensible part won because it was for her own good. Resolved, she sank into the nearest chair and reached for the telephone.

Chase's mother took the call at the nurses' station. 'Tasha? Is everything all right?'

It wasn't, but it soon will be, Tasha thought resolutely. 'I'm fine, Elaine. I just forgot to tell you something. I won't be able to see Chase tonight. I've arranged to go to a baseball game with a friend. It's his birthday, and I can't let him down.' She didn't know why she hadn't said that her companion was a schoolboy but, having omitted it, she decided that it was best to leave that area shady. She might have need of an imaginary boyfriend one day.

'Of course you can't. Chase will be disappointed not to see you, but I'm sure he'll understand,' Elaine responded promptly, though her voice seemed to say, I'm not sure I do.

Tasha refused to feel guilty. 'Tell him I'll see him tomorrow,' she added coolly, before putting the phone down.

Sighing, she made no move to get up though she had plenty to do. She had always thought that love would be a wonderful experience, but it looked like she was wrong. It was damned painful.

In the end she went to the game, determined to enjoy herself. There was no point in going around with a long face. Besides, she didn't want to spoil things for Stevie. As it turned out, she did enjoy herself in spite of everything. She loved baseball, and it was great watching with someone who got as excited as she did. There was something cathartic in shouting and cheering along with the crowd. And the hot dogs and sodas had never tasted better. For an hour or two she forgot her problems, and was as ecstatic as her small companion when their team came out winners.

'Gee, that was great!' Stevie declared as they joined the crowds spilling out of the ground.

'So you enjoyed yourself, Stevie?' Tasha checked, grinning because she knew the answer. If he had told her once he had told her a thousand times!

He grinned back up at her, showing off the gap where he had lost a tooth recently. 'It was the best birthday present ever. Just wait till I tell Mom!'

Tasha felt a moment's pity for her friend. Annie hated baseball, but she was a single mother and didn't want Stevie to miss out on anything. So she went to every Little League game and listened to Stevie's retelling of the match over and over because she loved him.

'Do you want to come in for some coffee?' Annie invited when Tasha dropped Stevie off an hour later.

Tasha had planned to refuse, but changed her mind. It might do her good to talk. 'Have you made brownies?' she asked, following Annie into the kitchen.

'Uh-oh, I smell trouble,' her friend declared with a grin that faded when Tasha didn't smile. 'It's got to be a man,' she sighed, spooning instant coffee into two mugs and setting a plate of brownies on the table.

'Why do you say that?' Tasha challenged as she sat down.

Annie uttered a dry laugh. 'Because only a man can make a woman look the way you do.' Setting one steaming mug before her friend, she took the other to a seat opposite. 'So, am I right?'

Tasha could have prevaricated, but she knew that she wouldn't be fooling her friend one bit. 'Yes,' she admitted evenly.

'Do I know him?'

Tasha reached for a brownie and bit into it. 'No, you don't know him.'

'Is he good-looking?'

In her mind's eye Tasha saw Chase's face, and her heart contracted. 'If you must know, he's drop-dead gorgeous,' she revealed wryly.

Annie propped her elbow on the table and rested her chin on her hand. 'What's the problem? Is he married?'

With a profound sigh, Tasha met Annie's curious gaze. 'He's engaged. To Natalya.'

Annie's jaw dropped. 'Your sister?' She had met

Natalya only once when she'd come to the office to see Tasha. Annie hadn't liked her.

After the briefest hesitation Tasha explained what had happened, and what she had done. To say that Annie was shocked was not to understate the case.

'Pardon me for saying this, but your sister is a bitch!' she exclaimed, shooting to her feet and taking a turn about the tiny kitchen.

'I forgive you,' Tasha pronounced, feeling the same way herself.

'When are you going to tell him about her?'

'Soon. Chase is improving daily.'

Annie bit her lip. 'Do you think…?'

Tasha pushed a hand through her hair and eyed her friend sombrely. She knew precisely what Annie wanted to say. 'No.'

'But you're so different from Natalya. Surely…' She halted when Tasha drained her mug and pushed herself to her feet.

'You can't make someone love you when they love someone else, Annie. Nobody asked me to fall in love with him. I'll get over it.'

'I don't know. I've never seen you like this before. I hate to see you hurting.'

Tasha glanced at her watch. 'I'd better go.'

They walked to the door together, and Annie gave Tasha a hug. 'You know where I am if you need to talk,' she said, and watched sadly as her friend climbed into her car.

Tasha was barely halfway home when she passed the sign for the hospital. She had fully intended to ignore it, but the further she went the stronger grew the urge to go back. She knew that it wasn't sensible and she was just asking for trouble, but some things were stronger than sense.

She battled with herself for a minute longer, but the decision had already been made. With a quick glance in the rear-view mirror, Tasha made a U-turn and headed back the way she had come.

CHAPTER THREE

THE hospital seemed unnaturally quiet as Tasha made her way to Chase's room. She halted in the doorway, surveying the room—which was in darkness, save for the small circle of light thrown by the lamp over Chase's bed. It was late, and his parents had obviously gone back to their hotel hours ago.

Walking up to the bed, she allowed herself the luxury of simply watching him. He had become so important to her in such a short space of time that it was scary. Sighing wistfully, she reached over to brush an errant lock of black hair off of his forehead and, before she could straighten, Chase opened his eyes and looked right at her.

'I knew you'd come,' he told her softly, with heart-shaking confidence.

Unable to look away from those magnetic eyes so close to hers, Tasha held her breath. 'You did?' she whispered. Lord, he was so near that she could feel the heat coming off him, and the male scent of him actually made her feel a little dizzy. In all her life she had never felt anything so intense, so overpowering, as their closeness. Her receptive nerves kept sending message after tingling message to her brain.

'Oh, yes. Ever since the accident there's been an electric charge in the air between us, Tasha. I've felt it, and I know you have too.'

Oh, she had felt it all right. She was feeling it now, but she knew that she shouldn't give in to the lure of it.

45

'Chase…' she protested, though to her own ears it sounded half-hearted.

'Aren't you going to kiss me?' Chase enticed silkily. 'You know you want to, and just the thought of it has been driving me mad.'

His words were pure temptation, and a trembling took hold of her as her gaze dropped to the mouth mere inches away. Chase wanted her to kiss him, and she wanted to so much that it was agony to deny herself.

Yet, with a flash of insight, Tasha knew that to kiss this man would be a mistake. A very big mistake. So far, all she had done was wonder what it might be like to be kissed by him. If she took up his invitation she would know and the knowing could be unbearable, given that they must part soon. If ever there was a time to be sensible this was it. Gathering the remnants of her common sense, Tasha began to form a refusal but the words died on her lips as her eyes locked with his once more.

'Tasha.'

Her name was a mere whisper from his lips, yet it seemed to Tasha that she heard him in every fibre of her being. She could not have moved if she had wanted to. Reason vanished under a barrage of yearning. Her only thought was that she needed to know. Hungered to know how those lips would feel; how they would taste. Her whole life seemed to depend upon it and, caught in a web as fine as gossamer and as strong as steel, her head slowly, but certainly, began to descend towards his.

The brush of his lips against hers was like a stroke of flame, and she caught her breath at the wonder of it. Chase inhaled sharply, drawing back the merest fraction to question with his eyes that they had both experienced the same incredible sensation. Soundlessly her lips formed his name and, driven by forces stronger than her conscious will, she answered by closing that gap and pressing her mouth to his again.

His hand came up to clasp the back of her head and hold her there, and the world went up in flames. Nothing mattered to her but that this earth-shattering experience should go on. She sank weakly onto the edge of the bed, forgetting everything save that the mouth locked to hers was giving forth pleasure like she had never known. Her heart was pounding madly. She felt feverish—hot and cold all at once. Blood zinged through her veins, revitalising nerves which made her tingle and gasp.

Only when Chase groaned in real pain did she pull away, breathing heavily and staring down into his grimacing expression. 'What's wrong?' Lord, was that really she sounding so breathless and passion-drugged?

'I forgot I was chained to this damned bed!' Chase gritted through his teeth. 'I tried to move.'

Tasha bit her lip. What on earth was she thinking of to act so carelessly? The man had broken ribs, and here she was draped all over him. 'God, I'm sorry. Did you hurt yourself?' she asked as she scrambled into a sitting position. She would have got to her feet, only his hand on her wrist prevented her.

One eye opened to glare at her. 'What do you think?' he barked, and she stiffened instantly, indignation welling up. She was damned if she was going to take all the blame!

'Don't yell at me, Chase Calder. There were two people kissing here, not just one. Remember you asked me to kiss you!' And what a kiss it had been! She would never forget it, and she felt that nothing would ever match it.

That brought his other eye open, and he was no longer glaring. There was an altogether different glint in his eye. 'Didn't I, though?' he drawled softly, scanning the flush on her cheeks and the bruised look to her mouth.

Feeling that look to her toes, Tasha braced herself to resist it—even as her nerves felt the magnetic pull of him. 'What does that mean?'

'It means I got rather more than I expected,' he informed her, and Tasha's throat constricted.

'You did?' God, why did she sound so pathetically breathless?

Knowing that he had her attention, the corners of his mouth curved upwards faintly. 'Uh-huh.'

Tasha glanced away to give herself a breathing space, then cast him a look through her lashes. 'How much more?'

He smiled reminiscently. 'Oh, about one hundred per cent,' he told her, and her eyes widened in surprise. 'That kiss was something else. It's never been that good before.'

His statement set her heart thumping again, but for a totally different reason. 'Never?' she prompted, needing confirmation of a possibility which was incredible.

Chase caught her other hand and locked his fingers with hers. 'Never. I don't know why but, since the accident, the buzz between us has been mind-blowing. I can't get a handle on it and, frankly, I'm not inclined to try. Something happened to me—to us—and it's all for the better. Not that I didn't enjoy kissing you before, but you've got to admit—this is better.'

The confession made her stomach contract with a spasm of fierce joy. It was unbelievable. Incredible. So earth-shattering that she could actually feel herself tremble inside. 'Yes, it is better,' she agreed with a breathless laugh. Lord, but she had to be careful not to give anything away until she had had a chance to think! 'It surprised me too.'

She watched, fascinated, as Chase's lips quirked with amusement. 'At least it was a pleasant surprise,' he said, unconsciously beginning a circular caress of her hand with his thumb. In doing so, he touched the engagement ring and raised her hand to study it. 'You decided to keep it, then?'

She must have looked as blank as she felt. 'Keep it?' Tasha queried, looking down at it in confusion.

'I could tell you didn't really like it. I thought you would have changed it by now,' he said matter-of-factly, and Tasha realised that Natalya would have favoured something more gaudy.

Not so herself. She thought it was a beautiful ring, one she might well have chosen herself. 'Actually, that wasn't it at all,' she denied, thinking fast. 'I was disappointed that it was too big, but I've had that fixed.' Providing he didn't ask for a jeweller's receipt, her lie was covered.

He frowned, clearly trying to piece what he remembered into what she'd said. After a second or two he looked at her questioningly. 'You like it?'

'It's beautiful,' she said honestly, and he shrugged and shook his head, probably putting the difference down to female quirkiness.

'I'll have to get the matching earrings,' he decided, smiling so deeply into her eyes that she had to take a deep breath to steady herself as that magic began to weave its way about them again.

Alarm shot through her at the thought of accepting further gifts which didn't belong to her. 'There's no need,' she prevaricated huskily, as his thumb took up that mesmerising touch.

'Perhaps we ought to change the subject, or I'll never get to sleep,' he suggested whimsically. 'Tell me about the ball game. I didn't know you liked baseball.'

How on earth he expected her to think when he was caressing her hand like that, she didn't know, but she tried to put some order into the mush her brain had become. 'I love it. I try to get to as many games as I can. Tonight we won, which pleased Stevie.'

The circular motion of his thumb stopped. 'Stevie?' he queried sharply

Tasha blinked at him. Lord, he couldn't possibly be jealous, could he? It appeared that he could from the frown he gave her. She wanted to laugh out loud, but bit her lip instead. 'Stevie is a friend of mine,' she said nonchalantly.

'So my mother said,' he grumbled, and this time she did laugh.

'You should see your face! Stevie is the son of my best friend. He's ten years old...no, eleven. It's gone midnight, so it's his birthday today. The game was my present to him. Satisfied?' she teased, and Chase pulled a wry face.

'Why you little...!' He made a grab for her but she held up her hands warningly.

'Remember, you're a sick man.' She warded him off with a laugh.

'Yeah, but I won't always be in this bed. You remember that!' he threatened, sending a thrill racing down her spine.

'Elephant is my middle name,' she riposted neatly, and the look he sent her promised vengeance.

'Next time you want to go to a ball game I'll take you,' he told her firmly.

'OK,' she agreed softly, and he groaned.

'I'm making a fool of myself, aren't I?'

Tasha smiled and bent down to press a gentle kiss on his lips, straightening and pulling herself free before he could react. 'Yes, but I like it. Now I must go. It's very late. I'll see you tomorrow,' she promised.

'I'll look forward to it. Goodnight, sweetheart. Drive carefully.'

'I will,' Tasha promised, and left him before she could think of a reason to linger.

At the end of the corridor she stopped and collapsed against the wall. Automatically her fingers rose to her lips and probed their sensitivity. She was trembling like a leaf, but she made herself calm down and go over everything Chase had said. She wasn't mistaken; it had been just like she'd thought. But she had come so close to missing it. If she hadn't turned back, if she hadn't kissed him, she would never have known!

She would never have known that what Chase experienced when he kissed her hadn't happened when he'd kissed Natalya. She wouldn't have known that the attraction which fairly sparked through the air whenever they were together hadn't been there before the accident. Which meant that whatever he felt was for herself alone. Natalya had never made him feel this way. She had something her twin simply didn't have; something Chase responded to. It was her he was attracted to so passionately.

So, what was she going to do about it? Her plan had been to tell him about Natalya in the next day or two, but now she was no longer sure. There was a new element in the picture, one she hadn't thought of. Chase wanted her every bit as much as she wanted him.

She now had two choices. She could tell him and, in all probability, lose him or say nothing, perpetuate the lie, and keep him.

No sooner had she thought it than her conscience smote her. Wouldn't that be morally wrong when he thought she was someone else? With a groan of despair she was forced to admit that it would be. Two wrongs did not make a right, and never would. She would have to tell him. Who knew, perhaps what he felt for her would be strong enough to overcome the fact of who she was?

As she pushed herself away from the wall and headed for the elevator she reminded herself not to hold her breath!

Tasha tossed her pencil down on top of her legal notepad and stretched. The action brought her eye level with the clock on the wall, and she received a shock. Disbelievingly she checked her own watch to confirm that it was almost seven o'clock. Where had the time gone?

Court had adjourned early but, having had a brainwave about another case, she had picked up a sandwich and coffee and buried herself in the library. She had made a mental note not to stay long but, as usual, the more she read the more she had to check and, before she knew it, the time had whizzed by.

That glance at the clock had told her that she was already an hour and a half late for her visit with Chase, and she still had to get across town. Heaven only knew what time she would get there. Or what mood he would be in.

Another ten days had passed since the accident. Days during which she had spent most of her free time with Chase—and hadn't told him about Natalya. Every day she had gone there, determined that today would be the day. He was improving by leaps and bounds, and could take the news. Yet every day she had put it off. She had no good excuse, only the fact that she was so crazy about him—falling more and more deeply in love the more she saw him—that she couldn't find the courage to tell him and lose him.

She knew that it was cowardly, but she couldn't help herself. He was everything she wanted in this life. She dreamed about him, erotic dreams that—when she woke—left her aching and unfulfilled. She thought about him all the time. Even her work couldn't block him out entirely. She found herself thinking of him at the most inappropriate moments, going off into daydreams and losing track of what was being said. Thankfully not in court, but on almost every other occasion. She was a hopeless case.

With a sigh Tasha shelved the books, gathered up her things and headed for the car park. At least the bulk of the traffic had gone by then, and she made good time across town after all. For once an elevator was waiting, and she stepped in quickly and pressed the button for Chase's floor. She paused in the doorway of his room and, as always, her first sight of him took her breath away. In silk pyjamas and dressing-gown, he looked unbearably tempting—bringing all her senses to a heightened state of awareness. God, it was good to see him. He made everything else seem unimportant.

As if sensing her presence, Chase looked up and saw her.

'Where the hell have you been?' he demanded crossly from where he sat in a chair by the window, newspapers scattered around him like a child's abandoned toys.

So that was the way the wind blew, she thought, tossing her purse and coat onto the bed and eyeing him with her arms crossed. He looked like nothing so much as a grumpy little boy, who had been waiting for a promised comic all day. Well, she was mucky, hungry and tired and in no mood for his tantrums.

'And hello to you, too,' Tasha responded sweetly.

His lips thinned. 'What sort of an answer is that?'

Her eyes flashed a warning which he inevitably ignored. 'The sort you get when you greet someone the way you did!'

Chase crossed his arms too. 'Don't try and put me in the wrong. Do you have any idea what time it is?'

Damn, but, to borrow a phrase, he looked stunningly attractive when he was mad. Her stomach clenched in response and she groaned inwardly. She didn't need this. 'I know precisely what time it is, thank you very much. I possess a watch.' She just hadn't looked at it soon enough.

'Then it wouldn't hurt you to turn up on time, would it? Where have you been all day?'

He was being unreasonable. She knew it was because he had a severe case of cabin fever but that didn't excuse him, in her book. She came every day, no matter what the weather or how tired she was after work, because she wanted to be with him, and he had the nerve to berate her because she was a little late! OK, more than a little, but that wasn't the point.

'I've been working, you big jerk! Earning some money so that I can eat and keep a roof over my head!' she snapped back, at the end of her tether.

'Working? At this hour?' he scoffed, and something in the way he said it made her pause before answering.

'What do you think I was doing, Chase?' she asked dulcetly, as cutting as a lancet.

'For all I know, you could have been having an affair!' Chase exploded, his jaw clamped so tightly that it looked painful.

She stared at him in amazement. 'You've got to be joking!'

'Why? Any red-blooded man would take one look at you and want you in his bed!' Chase countered, leaving her wavering between bemusement that he saw her as some kind of *femme fatale* and anger.

Anger won. 'Let me tell you something, Chase Calder. I am not some mindless bimbo. I do not fall over for any man who wants me! Nor do I happen to want any man but you. Though God knows why, when you can imagine that I would do such a thing!'

Chase went still, and Tasha was fascinated to see a tide of colour rise up his neck. 'Are you telling me I'm wrong?'

That he needed to ask kept her fuse lit. 'I've a good mind to come over there and hit you!'

Chase let out his breath in a heavy sigh and rubbed a hand round his neck. When he looked at her again his expression was rueful. 'You're angry.'

Tasha rolled her eyes. No kidding! 'I think I have a right to be, don't you? I've just had one hell of a day in court, and then you have the nerve to suggest...' She cut the rest off as she saw the surprise on his face.

'Court?' he queried, and she realised that she had just stepped into that minefield again. Odd as it might seem, her work hadn't come into any of the conversations they had had and, apparently, his parents hadn't mentioned it either.

Now she was left, wondering what Natalya had told him. For herself, she had to tell the truth. 'Yes, I'm a lawyer,' she announced, and waited with bated breath for his reaction.

Chase was frowning. 'I thought you were a secretary,' he informed her, and her heart sank. There was a great difference between a secretary and a lawyer. How could she explain that away?

The angry colour drained out of her cheeks. All she could do was bluff. 'I don't remember saying any such thing,' she responded, telling him the absolute truth and hoping that he would miss the way her voice shook faintly.

Much to her amazement, Chase suddenly looked discomfited. 'You didn't. I naturally assumed that when you said you worked in a law office you were a secretary,' he informed her shortly.

It sickened Tasha to realise that not only had her sister appropriated her name she had hijacked her profession too. Not exactly, because she couldn't have got away with pretending to be a lawyer, but close enough. No doubt she had thought it would make her more acceptable to Chase. Thankfully, between her sister's lie and Chase's assumption, there was room for her to manoeuvre. He was about to discover that she was a different person.

'I thought a lawyer knew better than to make assumptions?' she rejoined, chin raised aggressively, and Chase's grey eyes suddenly caught light.

'I stand corrected, but I plead mitigating circumstances,' he said evenly, his eyes never leaving her face.

The look in his eyes could have started a brush fire. It certainly heated up her blood and set her nerves dancing. It took all of her aplomb to hide her reaction. 'What mitigating circumstances?' she charged doubtfully, and he started to smile.

'When I'm with you I tend not to think clearly.'

Second that emotion! she thought wryly. With a heavy sigh, her temper subsided. 'Sounds familiar. As to why I'm late, I got caught up in research and lost track of the time,' she admitted ruefully.

Grey eyes danced with wry amusement. 'Now that I know all about,' Chase owned, and Tasha smiled conspiratorially. 'Did you win the case?'

Her eyes lit up with triumph, and she grinned broadly. 'Oh, yes.'

'No false modesty?'

Her chin went up. 'I'm good at what I do.'

Chase held his hands up, palms out. 'I wouldn't doubt it for a moment. What do you practise—criminal law?'

Tasha shook her head. 'Civil. I'll leave all the head-line-hunting to you,' she rejoined sardonically.

'You make it sound as if I seek out publicity,' he protested, and she sent him an old-fashioned look.

'From all accounts, you don't go out of your way to avoid it. I'd say your ego loves seeing your face splashed all over the press and TV.' She knew that it wasn't true, or she would have seen his picture countless times. But that didn't stop her seeking redress.

'Ego! What kind of man do you think I am?' Chase asked darkly, and Tasha gave a tiny gurgle of laughter. He realised then that she had been getting her own back and he groaned. '*Touché*. Does that mean I'm forgiven?'

Her eyes danced. 'It means I'll think about it.'

An excitingly menacing look entered his eyes and her heart lurched. 'Don't take too long,' he warned, and Tasha narrowed her gaze suspiciously.

'Why, what are you going to do?'

'I might change my mind,' he informed her airily, and she felt that electric tingle shimmer in the air around them.

'About what?' she queried, as the exhilarating tension began to set her heart tripping.

'That would be telling,' Chase evaded smoothly, and his gaze dropped to her mouth, making her lips burn as if he had really touched them. Right on cue, her tongue came out nervously to moisten her lips and Chase uttered a groan.

Tasha's stomach kicked, and her pulse galloped away madly. All at once she had to swallow in order to speak. 'You know, you can be so aggravating!' she accused irritably.

Chase cleared his throat. 'I know, but you love me

anyway,' he said hoarsely, and Tasha caught her breath, incapable of denying it even to shield herself from the hurt to come.

'A-are you going to tell me why you were so angry?'

Chase sighed and dragged a hand through his already untidy hair. 'Because I missed you, damn it.'

The admission turned her heart over. 'Oh, Chase!' she sighed helplessly, feeling the remains of her already crumbling defences shatter at those few telling words. She'd missed him, too.

He held out a hand towards her, a winsome smile curving his lips. 'Why don't you come over here and let me say hello properly?'

She didn't need more urging than that. When she took his hand her blood simply started to sing.

'You're too far away,' he declared throatily, and she obeyed the gentle pressure on her hand and sank to her knees beside the chair. 'That's better,' he said with satisfaction as he cupped her cheeks and tipped her head up so that he could study her. 'Hell, I thought we'd never be alone together. I've been waiting for this. I want you to kiss me properly, not give me one of those pecks on the cheek I've been getting lately.'

Tasha moaned softly, knowing how he felt. There had always been someone else in the room when they'd been together, and all she had been able to do was give him the briefest kiss. It had been so frustrating.

'I...'

A nerve flickered in his jaw as his eyes dropped to her trembling mouth. 'For God's sake, shut up, Tasha, and just kiss me. I've been quietly going out of my mind, wanting to know the feel and taste of you again!' Chase exclaimed passionately, and Tasha moaned again. She wanted it too. So much that it hurt.

'Chase.' His name was a sigh of pleasure as his mouth

took hers, and her hands rose to rest lightly against the warmth of his chest. She felt him shudder at her touch, and experienced an overwhelming rush of satisfaction to know that she could make him react that way. Which was the last thought she had for some time. Everything became sensation as he supped at her lips, brushing them with his own and nipping them softly with his teeth before stealing her heart with the brush of his tongue.

Her lips parted instantly, allowing him entrance, and it was just like before—only more so. His tongue stroked and teased, drawing hers into a dance so intimate that she felt a tide of heat scorch her from her head to her toes. Her hands curled into the silk of his pyjama jacket, holding on as the world spun and she whimpered her pleasure.

Neither knew what would have happened if the sharp clatter of metal from the corridor hadn't made them spring apart in shock. Her heart thumping crazily and breathing as if she had been in a gruelling race, Tasha sank onto her heels and simply stared up at him.

'Don't look at me like that!' Chase groaned helplessly, and when her lashes dropped obediently he groaned aloud and tipped her face up again. 'No, look at me any way you like. Those eyes! Hell, I can't get enough of you! Damn this room where you can't get a moment's privacy!'

Hearing him say what she felt brought a sigh from her bruised lips. 'I think I should be alarmed by the look in your eyes,' she told him with a husky laugh, arresting his attention.

One thumb brushed back and forth across her lips. 'And are you?'

Tasha's nerves danced crazily. 'No,' she sighed honestly, and Chase brought his forehead down to rest against hers.

'Do you have any idea how much I love you?'

She was glad that he couldn't see her wince. She had no idea how he felt. He was attracted to her, but that wasn't love. Yet it could become love and, if she was honest, that was what she was hoping for. That he would forget Natalya and love her. It could happen. The woman he was getting to know was herself. Slowly but surely she was wiping her sister from his mind. He liked the differences; preferred the person he saw now. One thing she did know was that in order to get love you had to give it.

'Could it be as much as I love you?' she whispered back.

With a reluctant sigh Chase fell back into the chair, turning his head so that he could watch her. 'I have a confession to make,' he said, and her heart turned over in sudden alarm.

'Should I be worried?' she teased, but found that she was holding her breath.

'No,' Chase said with a smile. 'If anyone should be worried, it's me,' he added, and Tasha let out her breath in a rush.

'Really? This sounds interesting. Tell me more.' She grinned at him, and he rolled his eyes.

'Just remember I'm a sick man.'

Her grin broadened into a smile. 'For a sick man, you kiss real good!'

An answering warmth flickered in his eyes and remained banked there. 'Don't distract me.'

'Sorry,' she apologised, unrepentant. 'I'll be good.'

Chase groaned. 'Not too good, I hope. Now, where was I?'

'You were about to confess.'

He pulled a face. 'Yeah, right. Well, the truth is, sweetheart, that when I met you I fell in love with the

way you looked. You're so damn beautiful I was hooked
before I knew what was happening. But now…'

Tasha's heart was doing a wild fling inside her, and
she tried not to leap to the conclusions she so much
wanted to hear. 'Yes? Now?' she prompted shakily.

Chase reached across to run the back of his fingers
down her cheek in a tender caress. 'Now I realise you're
even more beautiful on the inside, and I'm falling more
and more deeply in love with you all the time,' he finished with a hoarse honesty that stole her heart all over
again.

Catching her breath, Tasha rose to her knees and
threw her arms about his neck to bury her face against
his shoulder. She hadn't been expecting that. Yet, without any prompting, he had drawn the line between before
the accident and after. He had fallen for Natalya's looks,
but it was her, Tasha, whom he loved now.

'Does that mean you like what I said?' Chase teased
gently, sliding his hands into her hair and resting his
cheek on the silken strands.

Tasha laughed, raising her head and looking at him
with her heart in her eyes. 'You don't know what it
meant to me to hear you say that.'

He used a thumb to gently caress her lips. 'Oh, I think
I can guess,' he said gruffly, and closed the gap to kiss
her—not with scintillating passion but with a gentleness
that told of much deeper feelings.

They were smiling at each other when a hesitant tap
on the door made them both look round. Chase's parents
hovered in the doorway.

'May we come in, son? Or would you rather we went
away again and came back later?' John Calder asked,
eyes alight with humour and affection.

Tasha rose gracefully to her feet as Chase waved his
parents inside.

'Did you get it?' he asked his father mysteriously, and John Calder patted his jacket pocket.

'All signed and sealed, son,' he reassured his offspring. 'Have you told her?'

'Told me what?' Tasha queried, her gaze travelling from Chase's bland expression to Elaine Calder's excited one. 'What's going on?'

'Good, you haven't told her. I wanted to be here when you did,' Chase's mother exclaimed, making herself comfortable on the edge of the bed. 'Go on,' she instructed eagerly.

'Thanks,' Chase drawled humorously, and Tasha was about to explode when he finally looked at her. 'First things first. They're going to let me out of this prison on Monday.'

'That's wonderful news. Now you can stop harassing the nurses,' Tasha declared.

He sent her a telling look as his parents laughed. 'At least at home I can work, even if I'm not allowed back in the office yet,' he said with feeling, and Tasha's heart sank.

'You're going home to Boston?' She pressed for confirmation in a shaken voice, unable to hide her dismay.

'As soon as possible,' Chase acknowledged, then smiled when he saw her bite her lip. 'How long will it take you to pack?'

Tasha's heart seemed to be on a roller coaster—down one minute, up the next. 'Pack? Am I going with you?'

'Well, you didn't think I was going to leave you behind, did you? When I go you go. That means on the charter Dad arranged for the end of next week.'

Her mind was reeling. He expected her to leave in a week? 'But...my job, my things?'

Chase swore under his breath. 'I must admit I hadn't

taken that into account. Will the job be a problem? Will you have to give notice?'

Tasha rubbed absently at her temple. 'Yes, but with the leave I've accrued, and some finagling, I should be able to bring it down to a week,' she thought out loud.

'Good. As for your things, we'll hire a firm of professionals to pack them all and send them on.' Chase sorted that out in a flash.

Tasha felt slightly steamrollered. 'You've thought of everything.'

Chase's expression sobered as he heard the flat tone of her voice. 'Except for the fact that you might not want to go. You don't sound too happy about it.'

'Of course I want to go,' Tasha responded uncomfortably. She loved him so naturally she wanted to be with him. She just hadn't expected to have to make the decision so soon. Which was stupid of her because of course Chase would expect to go home as soon as he was fit enough. It was simply that she was being brought face to face with what she hadn't told him.

Unaware of her uneasy thoughts, the light returned to his eyes. 'Good, because there's one more thing.'

'One more?' Tasha couldn't think of anything.

'Yes, dear,' Elaine confirmed, drawing Tasha's attention. 'John and I had to delay our trip to Hawaii when Chase had the accident. We always go there for our wedding anniversary. As we were late, anyway, we decided it wouldn't matter if we put it off for another week.'

'Allowing us to be married here before they go,' Chase declared, stealing her breath away.

Married? Chase wanted them to be married? Of course she wanted that but somehow, in her mind, the event had been way ahead of them. She had imagined them living together for a while first. Vaguely, too, had been the hazy notion that before then, secure in the knowledge

that he loved her and only her, she would finally tell him
about Natalya. But she had been thinking in terms of
months, not days. Now she had just over a week.

She looked from his parents to Chase and was lost.
'Looks like I'll have to find a dress in a hurry, then,
won't I?' She gave her answer with a choked laugh.

Inside, though, she wasn't laughing. Time had just run
out. God help her, she was going to have to tell him and
hope that what he felt for her was strong enough to
weather the shock.

CHAPTER FOUR

TASHA had every intention of telling Chase the truth. She knew that it was wrong not to. However, finding the right time to tell him proved to be a great deal harder than she had expected, and she had never thought that it would be easy.

Chase left hospital on Monday and moved into a suite in the same hotel as his parents. Needing to leave the files on her cases in order for her replacement, Tasha worked late and didn't get to see Chase before that evening—when she had arranged to have dinner with him and his parents. Consequently, they didn't manage to be alone together until his parents had said goodnight and they escaped upstairs to his sitting-room.

Naturally, the last thing on either of their minds was talking, and it was a long time later when they reluctantly drew apart and allowed the real world to return.

'This suite must cost the earth,' Tasha murmured. Lying on the couch in the curve of Chase's arm and drugged by kisses which still had her heart thumping, she surveyed the elegant decor of the interior through half-closed eyes. Beneath her head Chase's heart thudded as wildly as hers. He had been the one to call a halt before matters had got beyond the point of no return. He wasn't fully fit yet, and the last thing they wanted was for him to end up back in hospital.

His hand began a slow caress of her nape as he looked around them. 'I can afford it,' he said matter-of-factly, bringing a tiny smile to her lips.

'Does that mean you're rich?' she teased lightly, not taking it seriously.

Chase laughed softly, a rumbling sound which set her nerves fluttering. 'I'm very good at what I do.'

Tasha didn't miss the quote of her own words, nor the message it conveyed. At the same time she remembered Natalya saying something along those lines, but she had hardly been paying attention. She concentrated now, though. 'How rich? Very or stinking?' she asked, keeping her tone light to mask her uneasiness.

'Stinking,' he told her gravely. 'Glad you're marrying me?'

Because of his money? Her first instinct was to defend herself indignantly, as he probably intended her to do. However, a second later the colour drained from her cheeks, taking indignation with it. That was what Natalya had been going to do, and she couldn't joke about something that disgusted her so deeply.

'I'm marrying you because I love you—not for your money!' she insisted emotionally.

'Hey,' Chase soothed, tipping her head up so that he could see her distress, 'it was a joke.'

She could never find it funny, not when she knew what she did. 'Not a very amusing one,' she levelled at him, and he sighed.

'I can see that,' he told her seriously. He caught her hand and raised it to his lips, kissing it softly. 'Sweetheart, I know why you're marrying me.'

Tasha stared up at him. This was the perfect opening. She should tell him now. Get it out of the way so that they could move on. But, even as she opened her mouth to speak, she hesitated. Doubts assailed her, burrowing insidiously into her heart and mind until she felt sick. What if she told him and he didn't understand? What if he couldn't excuse her deception? Worse, what if he couldn't forgive it? She would lose him. The awful possibility made her freeze up inside.

Never in her life had she known fear like this before. If she lost Chase... Desperately she sought to hold on to reason. She was fearing the worst because she felt so vulnerable. It might not happen that way. Yet it could, and her good intentions died a coward's death. She couldn't do it now. She *would* tell him, but she would wait until she felt more confident.

She reached up and pulled his head down to hers. 'I know you do. I love you, Chase. I love you so much!' she declared passionately, and kissed him almost desperately.

Within seconds Chase was responding. The world drifted away, and the opportunity was lost for ever.

Another two days went by, during which Tasha berated herself for her cowardice. Logic told her that it would make things worse to wait, yet it was so hard to be logical when her emotions were involved.

On Wednesday they met up with Chase's parents for lunch to discuss the details of the wedding. His mother was determined to make it an occasion, despite the short notice.

'Alison and her husband, Matt, are flying in, and Evan has promised to be here,' Elaine Calder remarked over coffee.

'I managed to stop her taking over a 747 and flying out the whole family,' her husband teased warmly.

'Oh, John, don't exaggerate so!'

'I wasn't,' he returned, and she turned a shoulder on him in exasperation.

'Are you sure there isn't anyone else you want to invite to the wedding?' Elaine asked, studying Tasha's short list of names.

'Only Annie and Stevie,' she confirmed, trying to enter into the spirit of the thing—but it was hard, with her conscience nagging at her.

'No parents?' the other woman queried sympathetically.

That was coming too close to home, and Tasha hastily cut her off. 'We were orphaned at a very young age,' she returned without thinking, and felt a jolt of alarm go through her when Chase instantly picked up on the slip.

'We?'

Tasha's stomach took a nose dive, and her heart gave a sickening thud. 'I...do have a sister,' she said carefully. She hadn't wanted to reveal even that much but, having been forced to by her own error, she realised that yet again she had an opening to tell the truth.

Elaine appeared delighted. 'Well, then, surely...'

'We don't get on,' Tasha interrupted quickly. 'In fact, I have no idea where she is.' That was true, even if she'd lied about the exact nature of their relationship.

'I'm sorry, sweetheart, that's too bad,' Chase commiserated as he reached for her hand, accepting her statement without question.

Tasha felt that she ought to say more, not leave the subject floating like this. 'We're not very alike. Not in how we think and feel. Rather like chalk and cheese, really.'

'What happened to you and your sister, Tasha? Were you adopted?' John Calder enquired kindly.

She shook her head, remembering how she had longed to be adopted when she was small but it had never happened. 'No. They didn't want to split us up and, at the time, there wasn't a family prepared to take the two of us. We went through a series of foster homes until we were old enough to leave and get a place of our own.'

'Coming from a close-knit family, I find it hard to

imagine what that must have been like,' Chase confessed, and she smiled.

'Sometimes it wasn't too bad,' she admitted, recalling that there hadn't been too much love. Oh, they had been well fed and well clothed, but emotional needs had somehow got lost in the process.

'But sometimes it wasn't too good either, hmm?' he guessed.

She acknowledged that with a shrug. 'Things improved when I went to college, then law school.'

'And when was the last time you saw your sister?' Elaine asked innocently, opening the door for Tasha.

She knew she should say, At Chase's bedside a few days ago, but somehow the words would not come out of her throat.

'I don't think that's something Tasha wants to talk about,' Chase observed, coming to her rescue.

Like a coward, Tasha followed his lead. 'We didn't exactly part on the best of terms,' she confirmed uncomfortably.

Squeezing her hand, Chase changed the subject and his parents followed suit, leaving her to cringe inwardly at her second failure to do the right thing. They chatted for a while then the Calders excused themselves, leaving Tasha and Chase alone at their secluded table in the restaurant.

Chase sent her an apologetic look. 'Sorry about my mother. She's interested in people and sometimes she isn't as tactful as she would like.'

Still feeling uncomfortably guilty, Tasha rested her elbows on the table and leant her chin on her linked fingers. 'I didn't mind. Your parents have been wonderful to me.'

'They like you, which isn't difficult,' he informed her with a lazy smile.

'I would have liked them for my own parents,' Tasha said softly.

Chase reached across the table and took her hand. 'Poor little Tasha.'

A flash of anger caught her unawares. 'Don't pity me, Chase!' she snapped, making an attempt to pull free—which failed under his superior strength. She knew she was overreacting, due to her own guilty conscience, but couldn't seem to help it. Sometimes she didn't seem to recognise herself at all in the emotional creature she had become.

'Pity is the last emotion you bring out in me, Tasha,' Chase shot back. 'Yes, I felt sad—but for the little girl who was so obviously lonely, despite the fact she had a sister. When it comes to the woman I'm looking at, pity is the last thing on my mind,' he added thickly, and it only took the briefest look into his eyes to know exactly what he meant. Colour stole into her cheeks as her blood heated up in response. All at once it was the last thing on her mind too.

'Oh,' she said inadequately, and Chase groaned expressively.

'Exactly.'

Tasha was silent for a moment or two, trying to compose nerves that wanted to riot. 'I think this is my cue to say I'd better go home to bed,' she said at last, and bit her lip when he laughed drily.

'Any mention of bed is likely to send my blood pressure soaring.'

Her response to him was so hot and immediate that it felt as if her own blood pressure was already in the stratosphere. 'I can't do anything about that,' she returned, and he sent her a scorching look.

'Not here, anyway,' he quipped, with a glance around the restaurant.

Tasha laughed, but her throat tightened. 'Perhaps…'

'Yes? Perhaps?' he prompted, and she closed her eyes.

'Perhaps you'd better start telling me about your childhood,' she suggested breathily. 'Start with the day you were born.'

'Trying to get my mind off the subject?' he drawled with raised eyebrows, and Tasha lifted her lids and gave him the benefit of the banked fires in her own eyes.

'No, my own,' she told him tautly, holding his gaze, and saw him swallow…hard.

Chase sank back in his own seat and closed his eyes briefly before giving her an oblique look. 'Let me see. I was born on a Thursday…' he began and, smiling faintly, she sat back and listened to the hypnotic sound of his voice.

Lord, was it any wonder she was so terrified of losing him? He was the most perfect man she could ever have dreamed of. How on earth was she going to tell him? How on earth could she not?

It was a dilemma which haunted her all through her last day at the office on Thursday. She hadn't expected the small party they threw for her at lunchtime, nor the brightly wrapped gift. It reminded her how happy she had been while working there, and part of her was sad to leave.

Yet the reality of her actions didn't become clear until she was getting ready for dinner with Chase hours later. She had already slipped into her black evening dress, and was admiring the way the full skirt flowed over her hips to just above her knees and how the yoke and long sleeves of lace added a touch of fragility, when the truth struck.

By resigning her job, accepting the good wishes and gifts of her colleagues and agreeing to marry Chase tomorrow she had already conceded that her future lay with him. Not that *perhaps* her future lay with him but, without question, that it did. Which meant that there was only one possible course of action she would take.

Motionless, she stared at her reflection and it was as if it spoke to her.

'You're not going to tell him, are you?' it accused, and she read the answer in her own eyes.

No, she wasn't going to tell him. She couldn't. All her life she'd been empty and wanting. Wanting something she hadn't been able to describe. Yet she knew that she had found it in the love she had for Chase Calder. She was absolutely terrified of losing him.

She would rather face anything than that. Logic didn't come into it. She couldn't risk losing him, and that was what could happen if she told him about Natalya. OK, so the alternative was a risk, too, but if she didn't tell him about her twin there was no way he would ever find out. Natalya would be thousands of miles away. Chase need never know that he had met her first. As the saying went, ignorance was bliss.

It was a reckless gamble. The kind of thing she had never contemplated doing before. Maybe it wasn't honest, but she couldn't lose him. She knew she could be storing up more trouble than she could handle, but it was worth the risk. Loving Chase was worth any risk, except the possibility of losing him.

The doorbell rang, startling her, and she swallowed nervously, smoothing her skirt with exaggerated care. Her mind was made up, and there was no turning back. With a final glance in the mirror, she picked up her purse and a silk shawl and went to answer the door.

Chase stood there, looking stunning in black dinner suit and white silk shirt. Silently he took in her dress and a smile curved his lips, even as a flame flickered to life in the back of his eyes.

'I see we had the same idea,' he murmured seductively, sending a shiver of awareness through her.

'What idea was that?' she asked breathlessly, not caring that he heard it and knew the cause. She had wanted tonight to be special, which was why she had chosen this particular dress.

'That we dine in the privacy of my suite. Unless you have any objections?'

He knew that she didn't but he wanted to hear her say it. 'None that I can think of,' she confirmed huskily, holding his gaze though it seared her and started fires of her own.

He held out his arm to her. 'The cab's waiting,' he said and, closing her door behind her, she slipped her hand into the crook of his elbow. They both knew the idea he hadn't mentioned was that they would make love tonight.

What she ate that evening, sitting at a candle-lit table by the window while soft music issued from the sound system, Tasha could never remember. She couldn't even recall what Chase had said to her. What she never forgot was how he'd looked. A bomb could have gone off right next to her, and she still wouldn't have taken her attention from him.

She loved the way he laughed with his eyes as well as his mouth. Loved the sound of it, and the way it rippled along her nerves. Enthralled, she watched the play of light from the candles on his face as he talked. He was so precious to her that it hurt. Her heart felt so full of emotion that she was amazed it hadn't exploded.

Tasha wasn't aware of the moment he stopped speaking and simply looked at her, a faint smile curling the edges of his lips. 'Have you heard a word I've said?' he asked with an indulgent laugh, and she came back to attention with a start, blinking at him.

'What?'

'I asked if you'd heard what I said,' he repeated.

'Every word,' Tasha confirmed, and Chase's eyebrow quirked upwards.

'What did I say?'

Her smile slowly blossomed. 'I haven't a clue,' she confessed unrepentantly, making him smile back at her.

'That's what I thought,' he returned sardonically. 'Did you enjoy the fish?'

Tasha stared at him blankly. 'Fish?' What...? Glancing down at her dirty plate, she realised what he was referring to. 'Oh, fish! Yes, it was lovely.'

Chase shook his head woefully. 'It was steak,' he told her in amusement and watched as her lips formed a silent O. 'I could have fed you on burgers and fries, couldn't I?'

Tasha didn't care that he was laughing at her. Tonight she only had eyes for him. Nothing else in the world mattered but him, and the thought brought with it a sudden anxiety. Her blue eyes locked with his.

'Chase, promise me you'll never forget that I love you,' she said urgently, causing him to frown.

'Are you planning on going somewhere?' he asked humorously, and she caught her breath.

'Why do you say that?'

'Because you sounded as if you were leaving me,' Chase said, with a plain question in his calm voice.

She'd never meant to give that impression, and she reached across the table for his hand. 'Never! I could never leave you. The only way you would ever be rid of me is if you threw me out.'

His fingers closed around hers. 'That would be like throwing away the best part of me, and could never happen. I know you love me, Tasha. Nothing will ever make me forget that.'

'Promise.'

'I promise,' he said solemnly, and she let out a shaky breath.

'You must think I'm an idiot,' she declared wryly.

'I think you're the most wonderful woman I've ever met, and when I place my ring on your finger tomorrow I'll be the happiest man alive,' Chase told her with such a depth of emotion in his voice that it twisted her heart.

'And I'll be the happiest woman,' she confirmed, her heart in her eyes for him to see. His fingers tightened around hers as he cleared his throat.

'Dance with me,' he urged huskily, rising and drawing her to her feet.

They walked to the centre of the room, and Tasha went into his arms with a sigh of pleasure. They moved slowly, her head resting on his shoulder and his chin brushing her hair. This was where she had longed to be. This was home. Nothing had ever felt so completely right before.

She closed her eyes as his hand began a slow caress up and down her spine, sending delicious tingles galloping over her skin. As they swayed together one strong male thigh brushed between hers, starting up an ache deep inside her. As if he knew, Chase's hand dropped to the small of her back and pulled her closer—close enough for her to discover the answering arousal of his own body. Her stomach clenched fiercely and her eyelids felt inordinately heavy when she raised them, her darkening eyes meeting the sizzling passion in his own grey depths. Holding her gaze, he brought the hand he held to his lips—drawing her finger into the moist cavern of his mouth and circling it with his tongue.

Tasha's heart leapt, her lashes dropping until she was

watching him through the merest slit. She could hear her heart racing and her breath catching in her throat. Her skin was alive with shivering expectancy and her breasts ached, her nipples hardening to push against the restriction of her clothing. She wanted him to touch her. She wanted to feel his hands and lips on flesh which cried out for his caress.

But Chase was in no hurry. He abandoned her hand and cupped her flushed cheek, lowering his head to let his lips taste hers. Brushing, teasing, he drove her to the edge of despair before his tongue finally traced her lips. They parted to him at once and a whimper forced its way from the back of her throat as his tongue plunged inside, claiming her.

Heat exploded inside her at each stroke of his tongue against hers and her fingers slid up his nape and into his hair, curling tightly as she responded. Kiss followed euphoric kiss, their tongues duelling, arousing—miming the act which both wanted.

By the time Chase dragged his lips from hers with a moan Tasha was trembling with need, her legs so weak that only his arm around her was holding her up. Breathing raggedly, they stared into each other's eyes and, with a groan, Chase swept her up into his arms.

Sanity returned for a moment. 'Chase! No! Remember you've been ill!' Tasha exclaimed fearfully, but he only held her more tightly and smiled down at her with a fierce passion.

'You'll just have to be gentle with me,' he gritted out, and carried her through to the bedroom, thrusting the door shut with his foot.

Setting her on her feet again beside the bed, Chase shrugged off his jacket and tossed it aside. His tie disappeared, followed instantly by shoes and socks, but he only managed to undo a couple of shirt buttons before he was reaching for her again—capturing her mouth in a kiss that left them both breathless. With a groan he found the zip of her dress and released it, his hands splaying out across the silky skin and branding her with the heat of his touch.

Wanting the same freedom to touch, Tasha reached for the remaining buttons of his shirt but Chase pulled away, taking her hand as he moved to sit on the edge of the bed and drawing her between his knees.

Standing above him, Tasha watched dazedly as he reached up for the edges of her dress and began to peel it downwards. Her heart went crazy, tripping over itself as finally her breasts were released to his heated gaze. Her teeth closed on her lip, biting back a groan as he buried his head in the scented valley between the jutting peaks. When her arms were free and the dress a black pool at her feet her hands went to his head and her fingers sank into the silky strands, clutching tightly as she held him to her.

'You're so beautiful,' Chase groaned thickly, breathing in her heady perfume.

Then, as she had so longed for him to do, he moved away just enough to enclose her breasts in his hands. Her head fell back as he moulded her, his thumbs rubbing over the aching tips and sending shock waves to the heart of her—making her clench her stomach with desire and deepening the already throbbing ache between her legs. She moaned, rocking her hips in silent entreaty, and when, in response, his mouth replaced his hand to draw her nipple deep inside where his tongue laved her engorged flesh the pleasure was so great that she called out his name achingly.

He treated her other breast to the same delicious torture before he slowly blazed a trail of kisses down over her stomach, setting her nerves fluttering as his tongue-tip probed her navel before moving on. His hands glided to her hips, finding the lacy edge of her panties and easing them down and away. Her mind went into dizzying shock when his hands closed over her buttocks, holding her to him while his tongue probed the triangle of hair at the apex of her thighs and found the nub of her pleasure.

One touch was enough to buckle her legs, and she sank to her knees. Gasping, Tasha found her head pressed against his chest. The scent of him tantalised her senses, and the heat coming off him scorched her. Beneath her ear his heart thudded wildly, and against her belly she could feel the strength of his arousal. It spurred her on to touch him as he had touched her, and this time he didn't prevent her. She was aware of his hot gaze as he watched her deal with the buttons and thrust his shirt open.

Lord, but he was beautiful—his shoulders broad and tanned, his chest firm and covered with a dusting of dark hair. She scarcely remembered peeling the shirt off and tossing it aside. The memory was lost when her hands finally closed on his chest, seeking out the planes of it and discovering the flat male nipples in their nest of hair. Her thumbs flicked them and Chase uttered a mind-blowing moan as he shuddered.

It was heady to know that she could drive him as crazy as he had driven her and, following his lead, she dipped her head and replaced her hand with her lips. When her tongue darted out to lap at him his hand found its way to the back of her head and framed it, holding her there until it became too much and he had to thrust her away. Breathing hard, they stared at each other— their passion a leashed wild thing whose energy shook the air around them. Finally her eyes dropped to his waist and the fastening of his trousers.

His belly flinched as he sucked in air at the first soft touch of her hands, but he did nothing to stop her making her own discovery. Tasha removed his briefs and trousers at the same time, her breath catching in her throat as his magnificent arousal burst free of his restraining clothes. Her eyes sought his, seeing the flush of desire on his cheeks and the tension in his jaw as he maintained a rigid control. When she reached out to fold her hand around his velvety hardness Chase closed his eyes on a groan.

'Yes!' The word hissed through his teeth as she stroked the length of him, but at the first touch of her lips his hand shot out to drag her away, pulling her up onto the bed beside him.

Passion exploded as they fell into each other's arms. The world became a writhing mass of entangled limbs as they exchanged kiss for kiss, caress for caress. Sighs turned to moans of pleasure and then pleas as they failed to get enough of each other. All was sensation, transmitted through slick, hot flesh, that stoked the furnace of need until Tasha felt she would go out of her mind if he did not take her soon. When he eased her beneath him and settled himself between her thighs she arched into him, desperate for release.

When he thrust into her she flung her head back with a cry of pleasure, lifting her legs to lock them about his hips as he began to move. She met his rhythm and matched it, hearing him groan as she took him deeper. The coil of tension expanded inside her, driving her ever up towards a goal she thought she would never reach, until suddenly she was there and the shattering intensity of her climax was so beyond her experience that it brought tears to her eyes as she held on tightly.

Seconds later she heard Chase groan and felt an indescribable joy as he, too, found release. He collapsed on top of her, but she didn't mind. She loved the feel of him, the strength of his presence. As far as she was concerned, he could stay there for ever.

Minutes later, though, he stirred and sighed, rolling onto his back and drawing her with him. His hand rose to stroke the damp coils of her hair.

'That was worth waiting for,' he murmured huskily. 'Though if I'd known it was going to be that good I would have taken you to bed sooner.'

Only then did it strike Tasha that Chase had never slept with her sister. She hadn't given it a thought before, but she was glad that it hadn't happened. She didn't know why Natalya had waited. It was hardly her usual style. Perhaps she had thought to secure him that way. Whatever, it had fallen to Tasha's advantage.

'All good things come to those who wait,' she teased sleepily, idly running her hand over his chest.

'And you are good,' he told her with a roguish laugh. 'In fact, you're very good,' he added then winced as she pulled a hair.

Smiling, she breathed in the musky scent of him. 'Actually, I was inspired, but your ego is too big already so I won't tell you any more than that.'

'You're inspirational, too. It's a good thing I'm not in hospital, or my blood pressure would have gone through the roof.'

'If you were in hospital this wouldn't have happened,' she pointed out, and grabbed a hand that was marauding in dangerous places. 'Stop it!'

'Now you know you don't really mean that,' Chase drawled wickedly, setting up shivers all over her.

'I do. I...' She caught her breath as he nipped at her ear.

Chase tilted her head up, his stormy grey eyes locking with hers. 'You were saying?'

'I forget,' she whispered back. 'I have a terrible memory. Did we just go into orbit, or was I dreaming?'

His lips twitched. 'You weren't dreaming, sweetheart, and it will be my pleasure to remind you exactly what happened,' he informed her, lowering his head.

'Oh, yes, please,' she croaked back, and it was the last coherent thing either of them said for some considerable time.

'Are you sure you're doing the right thing?' Annie asked as she watched Tasha put the finishing touches to her make-up. They were in Tasha's apartment. It was Friday afternoon, and Tasha was preparing for her wedding.

'I love him, Annie,' she replied simply, blotting her lipstick and sitting back to examine the effect. She had kept it simple, just some mascara and lipstick and a little blusher to put colour into her cheeks—though she hardly needed it after the hours she had spent with Chase last night and this morning. She had got home only a short while before Annie had arrived with Stevie.

'But if he ever finds out...' Annie left that hanging and Tasha stood smoothly, slipping her feet into cream leather shoes.

'He won't,' she declared firmly, standing in front of the mirror one last time. She had found the ivory silk suit in one of the more expensive stores. It had cost an arm and a leg, but as she only intended to get married once she decided that it was worth the money.

'I can't help thinking you're making a terrible mistake,' her friend sighed.

Tasha picked up the matching cream purse and checked that she had her important documents inside. Her cases had already been collected and taken to the airport. Whatever remained in the apartment would be packed and either stored, in the case of furniture, or shipped east. In little under an hour from now she would become Mrs Chase Calder.

She turned to her friend, who had agreed to be a witness, and silently begged her understanding. 'Maybe I am, but I have to do this. I've never been so sure of anything in my life. Can't you just be happy for me, Annie?'

'Aw, heck!' Annie exclaimed, defeated, and gave Tasha a hug. 'Of course I'm happy for you. I'll miss you, that's all.'

A loud knock sounded on the bedroom door. 'Hey, are you two ever coming out? I'm bored!' Stevie shouted, and the two women drew apart with a laugh.

Opening the door, Tasha did a twirl. 'What do you think, Stevie; will I do?'

Dressed in brand new shirt and trousers, Annie's son looked cute but uncomfortable. 'Wow!' he gasped in appreciation.

'Let's hope Chase thinks the same,' his mother pronounced drily, and shooed her son towards the door.

Tasha took one last look round the place she had called home these last few years. She had put a lot of love and hard work into it but she wouldn't really miss it. Everything that meant anything to her now was tied up in Chase Calder.

John Calder had arranged for a limousine to take them to the church. They were early and, superstitiously, Tasha had the driver go round the block again. Then they were inside the beautiful building, and she could see Chase waiting for her. Her heart lurched as it always did when she saw him. Any remaining anxiety left her at that moment. She loved this man. She would never do anything to hurt him. She would be the best wife he could wish for because she knew she could make him happy.

Half an hour later they were outside in the sunshine again, and she was no longer Tasha Larsen but Mrs Chase Calder. To prove it she had a gold band on her finger, matching the larger one which Chase now wore.

At the top of the church steps Chase paused and looked down at her.

'Happy, darling?' he asked, and she smiled up at him with the confidence of his love.

'Very happy.'

She would never look back. All that existed now was the future.

CHAPTER FIVE

TASHA watched her husband with patent enjoyment as he moved around the bedroom. Chase never ceased to stir her blood, clothed or unclothed.

In his dark business suit Chase looked lean and powerful, showing that he had fully recovered from that traumatic accident months ago. He needed a haircut, she mused. His black hair was just a little too long. Although she preferred it curling over the collar of his shirt it didn't fit his courtroom image. He wanted to appear incisive and indomitable. She had never told him that his mouth revealed a sensuality in direct opposition to that requirement. She was well acquainted with his hidden fires. Fires she was always ready to stoke and jump into.

His dressing complete, Chase came back to the bed and perched on the edge beside her. A rueful smile curled about his lips, and the warmth in his eyes stole her breath every bit as much as the brush of his fingers over her cheek and across her lips.

'If I didn't have to get to the office I'd climb right back in there with you,' Chase declared throatily.

'Can't I tempt you?' she taunted in a breathy voice, and loved it when he groaned.

'You're a menace. You know darn well I'll be thinking of you when I should be preparing a case.'

'Uh-huh,' she acknowledged with a grin, and he groaned again.

'I'm out of here,' he stated firmly, but he paused long enough to press a lingering kiss on her lips. At the door he shot her a look. 'Don't stay there too long. You've got a habit lately of staying in bed longer each morning. Don't forget you've a business to run too,' he cautioned her before leaving.

Minutes later Tasha heard the front door shut and a slow, cat-that-ate-the-cream smile spread across her lips. Happiness was an expanding bubble inside her. Now that Chase had left for the office she had the whole day to carry out her plans. She wasn't going to the small law practice she had opened up in the nearest town soon after they'd moved here. She had more important things to do. Her partner, a woman with a grown-up family, had cheerfully agreed to hold the fort for the day.

She rolled over in the large double bed, burying her face in Chase's pillow and breathing in the intoxicating scent of him. A little over an hour ago they had made slow, incredibly passionate love to each other. It had been initiated by her, but Chase hadn't been at all reluctant to follow her lead. Her smile grew at the memory. She'd told him it was his anniversary present. They had been married eight months to the day. Eight wonderful, perfectly happy months.

She had known she could make him happy and she had been proved right. She would never regret the things she had done because Chase loved her as much as she loved him, and tonight—when she gave him his real present—their happiness would be complete.

Too excited to linger, Tasha slipped from the bed and glided into the bathroom. She abandoned the idea of a long, lazy bath for a shower. Her appointment was for ten o'clock, and she did not want to be late. Ten minutes later, wrapped in a fluffy towel, Tasha returned to the bedroom to dress. Shedding the towel, she paused as she caught sight of herself in the cheval glass.

It wasn't her figure which caught her attention, but the soft swell of her abdomen. A hand went to it protectively, as if she could feel the life inside her. A life as yet unconfirmed, but which she knew was there. Her lips curved tenderly. This was her present to Chase. Their baby. He would love it—this visible proof of their love for each other.

Snapping out of her reverie, Tasha glanced at the clock and groaned. They had discovered this lovely old house in the heart of the countryside, and though it was perfect for the family they both wanted it was not exactly convenient. The journey into Boston could turn into a nightmare. If she wasn't careful she was going to be late. Donning filmy scraps of silk and lace underwear, she grabbed the first clothes that came to hand and struggled into them.

Several hours later, her pregnancy confirmed and loaded down with shopping, Tasha returned to the house. She had given Madge, their housekeeper, the evening off. Tonight she was going to cook their meal herself. She wasn't a bad cook, or a bad housekeeper; it was just that, with her tendency to get lost in her work, without Madge they would have starved and been buried under a mountain of dust!

Dumping the bags of groceries on the kitchen counter, she tossed coat and purse aside and made herself a cup of tea and some toast. Propped on a stool, she sipped the tea and breathed a satisfied sigh. Everything was perfect. Their life was wonderful. It proved that good could come out of bad. She had been accepted by Chase's small circle of friends but, more importantly, his family had taken her in and made her one of their own. She could imagine the look on Elaine Calder's face when Chase told her the news!

Of course, she had to tell Chase first, which thought made her glance at the clock and hastily reach for the shopping to begin preparing the food. She had decided to cook all Chase's favourite dishes. That would set him wondering, but she didn't think that he would guess her surprise. It was a labour of love, and she enjoyed spending the time on it. When everything was in hand, the table laid and a bottle of wine chilling in the refrigerator, she finally went to get ready herself.

Chase usually arrived home around seven o'clock, and she was downstairs again in plenty of time. She had chosen to wear Chase's favourite dress. It was the black one she had worn the night they had first made love, and had extra-special connotations for both of them. The prospect of his love-making had her dabbing perfume on all her pulse spots. She wanted everything to be perfect.

Tasha was removing the roast from the oven when she heard his car outside. Quickly removing the teatowel she had used to protect her dress, she took two cocktail glasses from the refrigerator and went out to meet him.

Chase didn't see her immediately, which gave her the opportunity to take in the sight of him. He always took her breath away. She guessed that he always would. She must have made some sound for he turned and saw her and she smiled, walking forward.

'Hi, can I interest you in a cold drink or a hot kiss?' she teased invitingly, waiting for the familiar glitter to appear in his eyes and his lips to curl into that lazy smile that sent shivers up her spine. She wasn't disappointed.

'Both, in reverse order,' he chose as he dropped his briefcase beside the door.

Setting the glasses down on the side table, she went to him, slipped her hands up around his neck and lifted her mouth for his kiss. It was languid, erotic and very, very hot, and when they eased apart both of them were breathing faster.

'I think I need that drink,' Tasha declared faintly, reluctantly moving out of his arms to get them.

'We can always take them to bed with us,' Chase suggested, one eyebrow raised enticingly. If she hadn't already made her plans Tasha would have agreed in a flash.

As it was, she shook her head. 'Can't. Dinner is almost ready. You've just got time to shower and change.'

For the first time Chase noticed her dress, and his face registered surprise. Then he caught sight of the dining-room, dark except for the glow of candles she had lit in expectation of an intimate meal, and his smile vanished. 'Are we celebrating something?'

Tasha could see his brain whirring as he tried to think of something he had missed, and she struggled not to laugh. 'Don't worry, you haven't forgotten my birthday. It's our eight-month anniversary, and I thought it would be nice to have a special meal. I've cooked all your favourites.'

Grey eyes grew sultry. 'Eight months, hmm? It feels like for ever.'

Her nerves leapt. 'A good for ever, or a bad for ever?'

He smiled. 'What do you think?'

Tasha took a shaky breath. 'I think you'd better hurry or you'll be eating burnt offerings,' she warned, and with a smile Chase headed for the stairs.

By the time he came down again the food was on the table. He collected the wine from the fridge and she watched him pour it, glad he had kept to the spirit of the evening by wearing a white silk shirt—unbuttoned at the neck— and the trousers of his dinner suit.

'To the most beautiful wife in the world,' he declared, raising his glass to her, and Tasha reciprocated.

'To the most handsome husband,' she said softly and they smiled into each other's eyes, before concentrating on their meal.

They were drinking coffee before Tasha finally

brought up the real reason for the meal. 'By the way, we'll have to get the decorators back,' she said offhandedly, and Chase frowned.

'What's wrong? I thought you said the house was perfect,' he pointed out—truthfully.

It had been perfect then, but not now. 'I don't like the colours in the small bedroom.'

Chase stared at her. 'We are talking about the bedroom for which you spent an entire month looking for just the right shade of green?'

Colour rose in her cheeks. 'Guilty as charged,' she riposted. 'I did do that, but now it's all wrong.'

Chase took a deep breath. 'And what colour do you want it to be?' he said with amazing patience. She would have been spitting nails.

Her lips twitched. 'Pink or blue,' she told him, wondering if he would catch on. He didn't.

'Pink or blue? Don't you think you'd better make up your mind before we call them back? Or I might end up representing one of the men on a murder charge!' he declared with heavy sarcasm, and she couldn't blame him.

Tasha spread her hands expressively, begging his understanding. 'But I can't make up my mind because I don't know yet what it's going to be,' she said reasonably.

'Don't know what what's going to be?' he contested with a touch of impatience, and she began to smile.

'Not what, darling, who. I don't know whether it's going to be a girl or a boy.'

This time the message got through and she saw the shock on his face, closely followed by delight. Chase swallowed a sudden constriction in his throat. 'Are you trying to tell me you're going to have a baby?' he asked gruffly, and her smile told him all he needed to know.

He held out his hand to her. 'Come here, wife,' he ordered, and she rose swiftly, rounding the table, to find herself pulled onto his lap and into his arms. 'You wretch! Why couldn't you have told me straight out?'

This close she could see the sheen of tears in his eyes, and it made her own surge to the surface. 'I didn't know if you'd be pleased or not. We've never really discussed when to have children.'

'How could I not be pleased?' he challenged thickly, then shook his head in wonder. 'God, a baby! Are you sure?'

'I had it confirmed today.'

The look in his eyes was tender and loving. 'So that's why you've been staying in bed longer. Don't tell me you were having morning sickness and I never noticed?'

Tasha knew he wouldn't forgive himself if she had been ill and he had been too blind to see it. 'No,' she assured him swiftly, 'I wasn't sick. I only feel a little nauseous now and again.' Lifting her hands, she cupped his face. 'About the decorators. I wasn't really serious about having them in. If you've no objections I'd rather do it myself.'

'Only on condition you let me help.'

Tasha tucked her head on his shoulder, feeling happiness oozing out of her. 'Are you any good at it?'

Chase laughed, hugging her close. 'I've no idea, but it's going to be fun finding out. Now, Mrs Calder, can I interest you in some long, slow loving?'

She moaned softly, pressing her lips to his jaw. 'I don't know. Are you any good at that?'

'If you're pregnant I must be doing something right. Let's go and check it out,' he suggested gruffly and, rising with her in his arms, carried her upstairs to their bedroom.

*　　*　　*

They did a great deal of laughing and planning over the next few days. Chase had a tendency to treat her like a china doll until she got mad and told him she'd throw something at him if he didn't stop. After that, life settled back to normal. Her business was attracting a small clientele so she was kept busy, often arriving home only a little while before Chase. Madge, when appraised of the baby, always made certain that there was a healthy meal waiting for them whatever time it was.

The following Thursday Tasha was later than usual and arrived home to find a note from Madge, reminding her that she had gone to her granddaughter's prize-giving and that dinner was in the oven. Stretching tiredly, Tasha stowed her briefcase in the hall closet, draped the jacket of her navy suit over a chair and went to check on it. She had laid the table and was glancing through her mail when she heard Chase come in. Tossing the letters aside, she went out to greet him.

'Hi, busy day?' she asked, slipping her arms about his waist just as she always did, and was surprised to feel him tense. She glanced up at his unsmiling face and her own smile disappeared. Something bad must have happened at the office. 'What's wrong, darling?' she probed supportively, ready to listen to whatever disaster had occurred.

Something flickered momentarily in Chase's eyes before he smiled, putting his arms around her. 'Now what could possible be wrong, darling?' he said evenly, and kissed her with an uncharacteristic roughness which confirmed her suspicion that something had happened.

Her lips smarting from that bruising kiss, Tasha eased back as far as he would allow her and stared at him. The watchfulness in his grey eyes suddenly sent a shiver down her spine. She couldn't imagine why he was looking at her so fixedly. 'How do I know until you tell me?' she responded reasonably.

'How does anyone know anything? Friends tell me I have everything a man could want. A beautiful house, and an extremely beautiful wife who loves me.' He paused, spearing her on the end of a searching glance. 'You do love me, don't you, Tasha?'

Bewildered and not knowing where this was heading, she frowned at him. What on earth had happened today? Something bad enough for him to seek the reassurance she gladly gave him.

'Of course I love you. You know I do,' she confirmed quietly, and was even more confused when he abruptly released her. He was beginning to alarm her. 'For heaven's sake, Chase, tell me what happened today!'

'What happened? I met a prospective client, that's what happened,' he informed her with the strangest laugh, and walked into the lounge, went to the liquor cabinet and poured himself a Scotch, downing half of it in one go.

Following behind, Tasha watched him in consternation. There was nothing odd in meeting a new client. Chase was head of a large law firm, after all. But, unless the man had got up and bit him, she couldn't understand what would make Chase react this way.

'Does this client have a name?' she asked, thinking that might tell her something.

'Oh, yes,' Chase confirmed grimly. 'His name is George Terlow.'

'Terlow?' she repeated, perplexed. 'I don't think I know him, do I?'

'Not unless you know something about the movie business. Apparently, he has his own production company. He and his wife were ''doing'' New England when a problem arose, and he came to me for some legal advice.'

'I see,' she responded, not seeing at all.

Her response clearly amused Chase. 'Do you, indeed?' he challenged mockingly, but before she could protest that he was being unfair he was speaking again. 'By the way, you'd better set another two places for dinner. We're expecting guests.'

Thrown off balance, Tasha could only blink back at him. 'Guests?'

Chase smiled, but she was fully aware that it didn't reach his eyes. 'George Terlow and his wife. I thought you might find them interesting, so I invited them to dinner. Ah…' The sound of a car pulling into the drive reached both their ears. 'That should be them now.'

Though she wanted to force him to tell her what was going on, there was simply no time. Spinning on her heel, she entered the dining-room and quickly laid two more places before she hurried through to the kitchen. She hoped that these people liked meat loaf because that was all there was ready.

She cursed Chase for not ringing and letting Madge know and checked the amount of vegetables Madge had cooked, hearing the muted sound of voices in the hall. At least they wouldn't go hungry, but the portions would be small. There was little she could do about it, though, and, lingering only long enough to ensure everything was kept warm, she went in search of Chase and their unexpected guests.

'Ah, there you are, darling,' Chase said warmly as she entered the lounge. He took her arm and turned her towards the man beside him. 'I'd like you to meet George Terlow,' he introduced smoothly, and Tasha found herself shaking hands with a short, tubby man in his sixties, who was staring at her as if he had seen a ghost. 'And this is his wife,' Chase went on, turning her to face the couch, 'Natasha.'

That was all the warning Tasha got. She had expected to greet an older woman but the woman who sat calmly on the couch, looking a million dollars in a figure-hugging red dress, was the last person Tasha had expected— or wanted—to see. All colour left her cheeks. The world she had thought so perfect this morning began to crumble around her.

The only saving grace was the fact that Natalya looked as stunned as she was. 'Tasha?' she yelped, sitting up straighter, then shot an accusing glance at Chase. 'You never told me you were married to Tasha!'

Into this drama George Terlow's amazed voice piped up, 'Twins! Judas Priest, you're twins!'

'And both, apparently, called Natasha,' Chase drawled, sounding amused—but Tasha knew he wasn't. Her head turned towards him. He was furious. Coldly, savagely furious.

Tasha closed her eyes, telling herself that she would not fall apart. No matter what happened, she would not succumb to the horror chilling her. Opening her eyes again, she forced her frozen limbs to move towards her sister who, for once in her life, looked uncertain. Like Tasha, she found herself part of a scene over which she had no control. Chase was pulling the strings.

Tasha gave her sister a tense smile. 'I'm Natasha; this is Natalya, my twin. She just prefers to be called by the name, Natasha,' she informed the two men as she kissed Natalya's cheek.

'Holy Moses, how do you tell them apart?' George Terlow asked, fascinated.

Chase met Tasha's stricken gaze and smiled glacially. 'By their hair. Isn't that right, darling?' He sought confirmation he didn't need. His look told her that he knew that and much more.

Once again it was George Terlow, apparently oblivious to the tension swirling around the room, who spoke up. 'Yeah, you're right. How about that? But for the hair, you'd never be able to tell the difference. I mean, if one of them said they were the other, hell, who could argue?' he chuckled, unaware of the dagger he drove into Tasha's heart.

'Who, indeed?' Chase murmured succinctly and, as white as a sheet, Tasha flinched inwardly.

'I...I'd better go and check the dinner,' she excused herself faintly and hurried from the room, uncaring of how it looked. She thrust through the swing door at the end of the hall and stopped only when she reached the sink, her hands clutching onto the rim for support.

Dear God, he knew! Pain lanced through her as she acknowledged the chill intent behind the act of bringing Natalya here. He knew and he had wanted to punish her.

'OK, what the hell is going on here?' Natalya demanded shrilly from the doorway, causing Tasha to jump and spin round.

'I thought it was painfully obvious,' Tasha responded sickly, noting that her twin had regained her poise and didn't like what she saw.

Her hands on her hips, Natalya glared at her accusingly. 'What was the point of that little charade?'

Tasha took a deep breath, wrapping her arms protectively around her waist. 'Chase wanted to tell me that he knew I wasn't you,' she said bluntly.

'Of course you're not me! He knows that perfectly well,' Natalya exclaimed shortly, only to bring herself up short. 'Or does he?' She stared hard at Tasha, who dropped her eyes. 'My God! You didn't tell him, did you? You pretended to be me!' Natalya took a turn about the room, her brain ticking over wildly.

'No wonder he acted so oddly this afternoon. I expected him to be furious with me—after all, I had walked out on him—but, instead, he was shocked. He had no idea there were two of us. He thought I was you because you had told him that you were me!' She laughed. 'My God, and I thought he was being so generous, inviting us to dinner. I thought it meant he had forgiven me, seeing he had found someone else to marry. When he was really livid because he thought he had married me all along!'

Tasha winced and pushed herself away from the sink. 'If all you can do is gloat then go back in the other room!' she snapped. Picking up the oven gloves, she began to take the dishes of vegetables from the oven.

Natalya shook her head. 'Who would have thought it of Miss Goody Two-Shoes? You'll be lucky if you come out of this with a bean!'

Pushed too far, Tasha slammed down the dish she was holding and rounded on her twin. 'I don't want his damn money! God, you make me sick!'

Propping herself against the counter, Natalya watched Tasha bite down hard on her lip to stop it trembling. 'Well, well, well, I do believe you're in love with him,' she said with mock sympathy. 'You should have told him, Tasha. You know he's never going to forgive you, don't you?'

It was the one thing she was most afraid of, and Tasha pressed her hands over her ears. 'Shut up! For God's sake, shut up!' she shouted, driven to distraction.

'Anything wrong?' Chase's calm voice enquired from the doorway and they both spun round, Tasha's hands dropping to her sides.

'No, nothing's wrong,' she denied hoarsely, wishing

FREE GIFTS!

FREE BOOKS!

Play

CASINO JUBILEE

"Scratch'n Match" Game

PEEL OFF LABEL

PLACE LABEL INSIDE

CLAIM UP TO 4 FREE BOOKS, PLUS A FREE NECKLACE

See inside

NO RISK, NO OBLIGATION TO BUY...NOW OR EVER!

CASINO JUBILEE

"Scratch'n Match" Game

Here's how to play:

1. Peel off label from front cover. Place it in the space provided opposite. With a coin carefully scratch away the silver box. This makes you eligible to receive three or more free books, and possibly another gift, depending upon what is revealed beneath the scratch-off area.

2. Send back this card and you'll receive specially selected Mills & Boon® Presents™ novels. These books are yours to keep absolutely free.

3. There's no catch. You're under no obligation to buy anything. We charge nothing for your first shipment. And you don't have to make any minimum number of purchases – not even one!

4. The fact is thousands of readers enjoy receiving books by mail from the Reader Service™, at least a month before they're available in the shops. They like the convenience of home delivery, and there is no extra charge for postage and packing.

5. We hope that after receiving your free books you'll want to remain a subscriber. But the choice is yours – to continue or cancel, anytime at all! So why not take up our invitation, with no risk of any kind. You'll be glad you did!

YOURS FREE!

You'll look like a million dollars when you wear this lovely necklace! Its cobra link chain is a generous 18" long and the exquisite "puffed" heart pendant completes this attractive gift.

(Pictured larger to show deta

CASINO JUBILEE
"Scratch'n Match" Game

SCRATCH HERE?

PLACE LABEL HERE

CHECK CLAIM CHART BELOW
FOR YOUR FREE GIFTS!

P7GI

YES! I have placed my label from the front cover in the space provided above and scratched away the silver box. Please send me all the gifts for which I qualify. I understand that I am under no obligation to purchase any books, as explained on the back and on the opposite page. I am over 18 years of age.

BLOCK CAPITALS PLEASE

MS/MRS/MISS/MR _____

ADDRESS _____

_____

_____ POSTCODE _____

◆ DETACH AND POST CARD TODAY! ◆

CASINO JUBILEE CLAIM CHART		
🍒🍒🍒	WORTH 4 FREE BOOKS AND A FREE NECKLACE	
🔔🔔🍒	WORTH 4 FREE BOOKS	
🔔🔔🍒	WORTH 3 FREE BOOKS	CLAIM Nº 1,528

Offer closes 31st January, 1998. We reserve the right to refuse an application. Terms and prices subject to change without notice. Offer not available for current subscribers to this series. One application per household. Offer valid in UK only. Overseas and Eire readers please write for details.

You may be mailed with offers from other reputable companies as a result of this application. If you would prefer not to share in this opportunity please tick box. ☐

MILLS & BOON IS A REGISTERED TRADE MARK OF HARLEQUIN MILLS & BOON LIMITED.

THE READER SERVICE™: HERE'S HOW IT WORKS

Accepting free books puts you under no obligation to buy anything. You may keep the books and gift and return the despatch note marked "cancel". If we don't hear from you, about a month later we will send you 6 brand new Mills & Boon Presents novels and invoice you for just £2.20* each. That's the complete price – there is no extra charge for postage and packing. You may cancel at any time, otherwise every month we'll send you six more books, which you may either purchase or return - the choice is yours.

The Reader Service™

FREEPOST

Croydon
Surrey
CR9 3WZ

If offer card is missing, write to: The Reader Service, P.O. Box 236, Croydon, Surrey CR9 3RU.

NO
STAMP
NEEDED

to God that they were alone so that they could talk. But they weren't. Chase had seen to that. He didn't want it to be that easy. She would have to sit through this farce of an evening first. Which she would do with all the grace she could muster. 'Dinner's ready. If we don't eat now it will spoil. I'll take everything through while you show our guests where to sit.'

What followed were the worst few hours of Tasha's life. Chase was at his most urbane, entertaining their guests as if there was nothing wrong. And for them there wasn't—not even Natalya. His anger he reserved for his wife, and she knew that the moment the others were gone the nightmare would really begin. She did her best to join in, but she couldn't eat and dared not drink more than a small glass of wine for the baby's sake.

Natalya preened, secure in the knowledge that nothing was going to happen to her. She might not have been so pleased had she noticed the contempt in Chase's eyes. He saw her for what she was now, but that didn't make him think any better of his wife. On the contrary, as she had always feared, she knew he was comparing her to her sister. A gold-digger, if ever there was one, because a young woman was unlikely to marry a man like George Terlow for any other reason.

It was a relief when George finally declared that they had to go because they had an early flight back to the west coast next morning. Chase walked them to their car, but Tasha hung back. She waved as the car moved off, then turned back into the house. Wandering into the lounge, she stared blankly at the empty grate.

'Alone at last,' Chase drawled mockingly from behind her and, taking her courage in both hands, she turned to face him.

'That was a rotten thing to do,' she said gruffly, hating to see the cynical twist of his lips.

Grey eyes impaled her, glittering with an icy remoteness she had never seen before. Walking to her side, he brushed his knuckles over her cheek in a parody of the loving gesture he used so often. 'My sweet, deceitful wife. Did you honestly think I wouldn't find out?' he demanded chillingly, and Tasha felt her heart crack.

'Chase, please...' She didn't know where to start: how to begin to explain why she had done this thing.

'I asked you a question, Tasha!' Chase snapped, making her flinch. 'Did you think I wouldn't find out?'

She swallowed hard, wishing she could lie but knowing that she couldn't. 'Yes.'

Chase breathed in sharply, then brushed past her to go to the liquor cabinet and pour himself a drink. He downed most of it before he looked at her witheringly. 'How could I have thought I knew you? I don't know you at all!'

'That's not true,' she denied instantly. 'You know all about me.'

He laughed humourlessly, studying her tense figure. 'All I know for sure, my *darling* wife, is that you are a liar.'

Tasha took a ragged breath, trying not to show the way she was trembling inside. 'I only lied to you about one thing, and that was because I couldn't bear to see you look at me the way you're looking at me now!' she exclaimed desperately, brought to the verge of distraught tears by the awful sense of dread that assailed her.

Chase looked at her long and hard, his face set. 'And how *am* I looking at you, Tasha?' he asked with harsh mockery.

She held his gaze with an effort. 'As if you despise me,' she whispered brokenly.

His lip curled nastily. 'How perceptive of you,' he

sneered, and her blood turned to ice, her heart frozen inside her.

Pale as a ghost, Tasha shuddered. 'Chase, please don't do this. Please let me explain,' she begged, uncaring of her pride. What good would her pride be if she lost him?

'And what, my love, will you explain?' He used the endearment with cutting precision. 'That you and your twin are a pair of gold-diggers? I don't know which of you I despise more. Your sister because her avarice couldn't stand up to the thought of being tied to a cripple, or you because you were so clearly willing to take the chance!' Chase snarled, downing the remains of his drink and going to pour another.

'It wasn't like that!' she protested helplessly.

'Then what was it like, Tasha? Tell me. I'm agog to know!'

Tasha flinched from his scorn, dragging a shaking hand through her hair. 'It's true that Natalya was going to marry you for your money but, I swear to you, it wasn't like that for me!'

He raised a sceptical eyebrow. 'Really? I suppose you're going to tell me you took one look at me and fell in love with me?'

Her heart lurched anxiously. 'I did. That's exactly what happened.'

'Do you seriously expect me to believe you?' Chase asked coldly. 'If you can lie about your own family I have to wonder what else you've lied about.'

Tasha went quite still. 'I would never...could never...lie about loving you,' she insisted emotionally.

'Wouldn't you? Yet you found it so easy to lie about your sister. You said you didn't get on; that you didn't know where she was,' Chase said scornfully, and she took an impulsive step forward.

'We don't get on!' she insisted raggedly. 'Nat knows I don't approve of the things she does.'

'You say that as if marrying a man while pretending to be someone else is acceptable behaviour!' he chafed her, and she winced at the direct hit.

'I know it was wrong, but I was terrified of losing you!'

'Terrified of seeing your meal ticket getting away.'

Tasha shook her head vehemently. Her heart was beating so anxiously that she could scarcely breathe, let alone think clearly. 'That's not true! Can't you understand? I fell in love with you, and all I knew was that if I told you what Nat had done you would hate her—and you would hate seeing anyone who reminded you of her. You would look at me, but you wouldn't see me. You wouldn't see the person I am.'

'So you pretended to be her in order to get me,' he said coldly, and Tasha closed her eyes helplessly. He made it sound so sordid.

'It didn't start out like that. I was going to tell you the truth when you were well enough to take it. At that time I didn't think it mattered that everyone mistook me for Nat. But then I realised I had fallen in love with you, and I thought that if I waited you would get to know me.' She looked at him then, her eyes begging for understanding. 'And you did, Chase. You noticed the difference. The woman you met before the accident wasn't the woman you found after. You fell in love with that woman. You fell in love with me.'

A nerve twitched in his jaw as he looked at her. 'So why didn't you tell me then?' he demanded, not denying her claim but giving her little comfort anyway.

'Because I didn't think it mattered! I loved you and you loved me,' she said desperately.

'Why rock the boat when nobody would get hurt, hmm?' Chase finished derisively, and her heart broke as she was filled with a dreadful certainty. He wasn't going to forgive her.

'I've hurt you. I never wanted to do that. My only excuse is that I love you so very much,' she said, choked by tears she dared not let fall.

Chase closed the gap between them and caught her chin in his hand, bringing his face down to hers. 'You don't love me, Tasha. You don't know the meaning of the word!'

Tasha's heart palpitated painfully. 'Yes, I do! I do love you!'

He shook his head. 'You want me. I can't deny the passion, but that's not love. Someone who loved wouldn't do what you did. Wouldn't take the freedom of choice away from me.'

Her throat closed up as she began to see everything she had done from his point of view. She had made an appalling mistake, she knew that now, and all she could do was defend herself and hope that something she said would get through.

'I do know love. Love is being only half-alive when you're not with me. It's the joy I feel at the sound of your voice, and seeing the warmth in your smile. It's hurting when you hurt. Love is knowing there is no other place I want to be but with you,' she told him in a voice hoarse with emotion.

'Even knowing I despise you?' he challenged cuttingly, and pain seared her heart at his cruel words— words which were meant to hurt her as she had hurt him.

'Even then, because I know you do love me,' she countered thickly.

He let her go, turning his back on her, to walk to the window and stare out into the darkness. 'Do I? How can there be love where there is no trust? For I don't trust you, Tasha. I don't think I ever will again.'

It was a shattering blow, and she didn't know how she managed to stay on her feet. Unconsciously her hand fluttered protectively to her stomach. 'Does that mean you want a divorce?' she asked in a broken whisper, staring numbly at his rigidly turned back.

He faced her then, and his expression was so grim and cold that she shivered. 'That was my first instinct. I wanted to get as far away from you as possible. Then I thought of the baby.'

The room seemed to heave, and for a second she actually thought that she might faint. 'You want to take the baby?' she croaked in disbelief.

The look of disgust he sent her quickly told her how wrong she was. 'My God, is that really what you think I'm capable of?' he demanded icily, and her heart sank further.

Of course she knew better; it was just so hard to think. 'I'm sorry. I...'

Chase interrupted her pitiful attempt to apologise. 'I happen to think that a child should have two parents,' he told her shortly, and she caught her breath.

'You're saying we should stay together for the sake of the baby?' she asked faintly.

'I have no intention of giving up my child. I'll fight you if I have to,' Chase confirmed stonily.

'What about me?' She knew that she could fight him and win. Given her situation, most courts would find in her favour but that would alienate Chase even further. She needed to know if there was an alternative.

'I'm fully aware that if I want my child I have to take you. I'm prepared to do that, but it will be a marriage in name only. You will be amply provided for. You can be sure your meal ticket will be safe. You name your price and it is yours, but you have to remain here with the baby to get it. I think that's a fair exchange. An open cheque in exchange for my child.'

Tasha knew that she should throw his insult right back in his face. It was no alternative. If she left she would barely see him, and if she stayed she would be condemning herself.

'You don't have to make the choice now,' Chase declared, once more staring out into the night. 'Tomorrow will do.'

She hadn't known that she'd made up her mind until she heard herself say, 'I'll stay.' Then she wondered if she was completely mad—asking to be hurt more than she thought possible—but she saw no other way. She didn't want to take the baby and lose Chase. She wanted them both.

Chase's expression was grimly amused when he turned back to her. 'I thought you might.' He set his glass aside and headed for the door. 'In that case, I'll move my things into the spare room,' he said evenly and left her, standing there alone.

Collapsing into a chair, she rested her head back against the cushions. She trembled all over with the multitude of shocks she had suffered tonight. This was some sort of crazy nightmare, only she knew that she wasn't going to suddenly wake up. Her heart was bruised and her emotions battered but, unbelievably, she saw one tiny ray of hope. Chase hadn't said that he no longer loved her.

She knew that she had hurt him very badly, and because of it he no longer trusted her. The greater part of a marriage was built on trust. She had lost so much ground that she didn't know if she could ever retrieve it, but she had to try because she couldn't believe that his feelings for her were dead. She loved him too much to just give in and accept that it was all over.

She didn't know what the outcome would be. She only knew that she had to stay and fight—because the alternative was too unbearable to think about.

CHAPTER SIX

HAD Tasha had any doubt that Chase had meant what he said the days that followed would have made it clear. Tasha hardly saw him. True to his word, he slept in the guest bedroom and left for the office before she rose. It was hard to accept, for she had become used to sleeping with him and found it next to impossible to sleep without him in the bed beside her.

Her appetite suffered, but she made herself eat because she had the baby to think of. To add to her misery, the morning sickness which she had scarcely suffered from previously now decided to make itself felt. Like so many women, she discovered that the nausea wasn't necessarily confined to the mornings.

It was a grim time, but she was determined to weather it. She hadn't known that it was possible to feel so lonely until Chase shut her out of his life completely. He arrived home late each evening, having presumably eaten out, and buried himself in his study for the rest of the night. If they did happen to meet he was unfailingly polite, but chillingly distant. She bore it because she knew that he had a right to be angry.

Only once did she attempt to break through the wall he had erected to keep her out. Sunday had always been Chase's day for relaxing. He had made it a rule never to bring work home, and they usually spent it doing something special.

She hadn't expected that, but neither had she expected him to bury himself in his study for most of the day. She knew why he was doing it, and it angered her. He didn't have to belabour the point. She knew full well that she was anathema to him. Yet, at the same time, his actions concerned her. It was all very well to punish her, but not at the expense of making himself ill. It was that worry that sent her along to his study that evening.

When he glanced up at her entrance she saw the tiredness around his eyes and her heart contracted. 'You're working too hard, Chase. There's a documentary on you might be interested in. Why don't you come and watch it with me?' she suggested hopefully. If he would only give a little maybe they could talk this through.

'I've too much to do,' he refused curtly, returning his attention to the papers on his desk.

Tears burned her eyes, emotional tears which—due to her condition—never seemed to be far from the surface. 'Would it hurt you so much to sit with me a while? I miss you,' she confessed tremulously.

'I don't recall any part of our marriage vows which said I have to entertain you,' Chase returned without looking up so that he didn't see her wince.

'At least stop working. I'm worried about you.'

He consulted a large legal tome. 'There's no need. I absolve you of any responsibility for my health.'

A spurt of anger shot through her. 'Damn you, don't tell me I don't have the right to care!'

He did look at her then. 'I assumed you wouldn't want to.'

'Oh, did you? Then you assumed too much!' Tasha fought to hold onto her temper and her emotions. 'How long is this going to go on?' she demanded.

Chase's expression was stony. 'I told you how it would be, Tasha, and you accepted that when you decided to stay. If my money isn't company enough for you then that's your problem, not mine. Now, if you don't mind, I'd like to get on,' he finished pointedly and, with impotent fury, she backed out and slammed the door.

After that she didn't try again. She discovered that she had some pride left after all.

Madge noted the lonely meals and the use of the spare room. However, the housekeeper didn't say anything until the following Thursday evening when Tasha came home from the office. As had become her habit, she went through to the kitchen in search of a cup of tea and some company. There was time enough to sit in lonely splendour in the lounge when Madge went home.

'You're starting to look downright peaked, my girl,' Madge declared as she set the steaming cup down on the table where Tasha was sitting.

'The joys of expectant motherhood,' Tasha joked, though she knew her pallor and weight loss were due more to the rocky state of her marriage than sickness. So did Madge, if her derisive sniff was anything to go by.

'Chase rang to say he would be dining out,' the motherly woman informed her tersely. 'Somebody ought to knock your two heads together, if you ask me. All this malarkey isn't good for the baby.'

Tasha pulled a face. She knew it and it worried her more, not easing the situation at all. 'You try telling Chase that. He's not talking to me.'

'I did. He told me to mind my own business,' the housekeeper stated drily.

'I'm sorry, Madge,' Tasha apologised at once, feeling guilty at having involved her in their problems. 'Chase has been working too hard and it's affected his temper.'

Madge gave her an old-fashioned look. 'I know what's affected his temper well enough. If you've had a fight make it up.'

Lord, if only she could! 'It's not that simple.'

'It never is,' Madge conceded knowledgeably. 'But you two love each other. It's as plain as the nose on your face. You've been as happy as clams. You'd be silly to let a stupid fight make you lose sight of that!'

That brought a lump to Tasha's throat. 'Yes, well, you might say we've run into a red tide so, please, can we just drop the subject?'

Madge opened her mouth to say more, but before she could utter a word the telephone started to ring. Tasha went into the lounge to answer it.

'Hello, Tasha,' Elaine Calder's cheery voice came down the line. 'How are you, and how is my grand-child?'

The sound of a friendly voice did Tasha the power of good, and she sank into a nearby chair with the first genuine smile she could remember for days. 'We're both doing fine,' she responded brightly. Elaine had been call-ing every few days since she heard the good news.

'Chase was concerned that the morning sickness was getting you down,' his mother revealed, surprising Tasha completely.

'He was?' she squawked, and could almost hear Elaine nodding.

'Oh, yes, dear. He rang me from work only the other day to find out if there was anything he could get for you.'

Tasha didn't know what to say. Chase had been so cold, so distant, that it was a surprise to hear that he was worrying about her. 'He never said anything.'

Elaine laughed. 'Well, you know what men are like. Big softies, only they'd hate for you to know it!' she declared.

Chase was certainly making sure that she didn't know it, Tasha thought wryly. She would have gone on think-ing that he didn't care, but for his mother. Now she knew he worried about her, and it warmed her heart a little. It was these small signs which kept her hope alive.

For the next few minutes the two women discussed various remedies. Only then did Elaine get around to the main reason for her call. 'I just wanted to remind you of the party for Evan and Isobel on Saturday. Don't forget you're both staying over for a few days.'

Tasha had forgotten, which wasn't surprising considering all that had happened. Chase's younger brother, Evan, was getting engaged, and they had planned to stay on for a short break. It couldn't have come at a worse time, yet she knew that it was impossible to cancel.

She made the only reply possible. 'We'll be there, don't worry. We'll probably travel up tomorrow evening and make the most of it.'

'That's wonderful, dear. We'll look forward to it. Oh, I'll have to go. There's a call waiting. I hope it's the caterer. Say hello to Chase for me, won't you? Bye now.'

Tasha slowly returned the receiver to its rest. She guessed that Chase had forgotten too. The party had hardly been on either of their minds in recent days. They could not get out of it, that was certain. She would have to speak to him about it. The big question was how?

She rang his office, only to discover that he had been in court all afternoon and had not yet returned. She left a message for him to call her, and spent the evening waiting for him to contact her. The telephone remained silent. The pettiness hurt, and if she hadn't needed to speak with him she would have said to hell with it. As it was, she retired to her bedroom and sat in bed, reading. It was almost midnight when she finally heard the car on the drive and, climbing from the bed, she slipped on her silk robe and headed for the stairs.

Chase was just locking the door when she reached the

head of the stairs and she paused, biting her lip when she saw the tired droop of his shoulders. In that moment he didn't look any more happy than she did, and her heart twisted. She would have gone to him if she hadn't been sure that he would reject her. Still, she must have made some noise for he looked up sharply.

Chase frowned and took a quick step forward. 'What is it, Tasha? Are you ill?' he asked, and she could hear the concern in his tone. It did her bruised spirit good, even if she had to deny it.

'I'm fine,' she reassured him in a husky undertone and descended a few more steps, only to falter when the concern was replaced with a chilling cynicism.

'Then what are you doing up so late? Or can I guess?' he drawled. 'Giving me a reminder of what I'm missing, darling?' he taunted, and a rush of colour entered her cheeks—partly anger, partly dismay.

Even so, Tasha refused to show that she was rattled by his suggestion. She gritted her teeth and continued down to the ground. 'I'm hardly likely to do something which would condemn me more in your eyes,' she pointed out staunchly, and caught his disbelieving smile.

'Need has been known to outweigh caution,' he returned mockingly, and Tasha felt her palm itch with the urge to slap him.

She resisted the urge. 'I have more self-respect than that. I'm here simply because I needed to talk to you. I left a message at the office. You should have called me.'

'I haven't been back to the office. And, as far as I'm concerned, we have nothing to talk about,' he declared coolly, not enlightening her as to where he had been.

Stung, Tasha folded her arms about her waist protectively. 'I'm fully aware that you abhor my company. Believe me, I wouldn't be here if it wasn't necessary. I promise not to take up too much of your valuable time!' she returned mockingly, salving her pride.

Chase clearly didn't care for her tone. 'Whatever it is will have to wait until later,' he said abruptly, and she ground her teeth angrily.

'When would you suggest? You leave before I'm up, and come home when I'm in bed,' she sniped derisively.

A muscle started to flex in his jaw. 'I've been busy on a case,' he told her frostily, and she laughed harshly.

'You've been deliberately avoiding me. What are you afraid of? What do you think I'll do?' she asked, and caught her breath when faint colour stole into his cheeks. She softened immediately. 'Oh, Chase, it doesn't have to be like this!' she urged, only to see him tense at once and his expression turn glacial.

'I don't have time to waste. Just tell me what you wanted to talk to me about.'

Feeling as if she had been slapped in the face, Tasha drew herself up. 'Your mother telephoned to remind us we're expected there this weekend. We're taking a holiday, remember?' She could tell by the way he frowned that he had, indeed, forgotten.

'I can't go. You'll have to ring and cancel,' he said shortly.

'I can't do that,' Tasha protested. 'It's your brother's engagement party on Saturday. He expects us to be there.'

'Damn it!' Chase dragged a hand through his hair, an act—though he didn't know it—which made him look sexier than ever.

Tasha's senses stirred. How she missed being able to touch him whenever the mood took her. She longed to do it now but she knew that if she tried it he would only reject her, and she wasn't quite up to coping with that right now. She forced her thoughts back on track.

'We have to go, unless you're prepared to explain to everyone just what's going on,' she said with a touch of asperity.

Chase shot her a dangerous look, and she held his gaze mutinously until he sighed. 'You'd better drive up on your own tomorrow. I'll catch the train on Saturday morning,' he ground out harshly, and Tasha caught her breath on a savage twist of pain.

'Can't you even bear to sit in a car with me?' she demanded, and felt the shaming welling of tears behind her eyes. Unwilling to let him see just how much he had hurt her, she turned to go back upstairs, but her foot got caught in her trailing robe and she tumbled to the floor with a tiny cry.

Chase was kneeling beside her in seconds and helping her to sit up, his expression suddenly full of concern. 'Are you OK?' he asked huskily, and her lips parted on a shaky breath.

'I've felt better,' she declared wryly. Their eyes met, and the stormy grey swallowed her up. Lord, she knew she wasn't wrong about him still loving her when he could look at her like that! He might not want to admit it, but it was all still there within reach. All she had to do was close the tiny gap between them and...

Chase clearly got the same message for he moved away from her physically and mentally, helping her to her feet with a detachment that twisted her heart. Then, having seen her safely onto her feet, he put the width of the hall between them.

'Before you break a leg,' he informed her tersely, 'it so happens I have a witness to interview on Saturday morning. He's vital to the case I'm working on, and unfortunately I can't beg off because he's likely to cut and run. Which is why I suggested that you travel up tomorrow, and I'll catch the train as soon as I can.'

One look at his face told her that it was true. Cursing herself for overreacting—though it was hardly surprising, given the circumstances—Tasha grimaced. 'I see. I'll pack a case for you, then, shall I?'

'I should be grateful if you would,' he responded evenly, and Tasha glared at him.

'There's no need to be grateful. It's the sort of thing a wife does for her husband,' she snapped, and he raised an eyebrow at her.

'We're hardly the conventional husband and wife,' he pointed out coldly. 'And, while we're on the subject, I trust you'll say nothing about our problems to my parents.'

Tasha knew that she had brought this on herself, but that didn't stop it hurting. 'We're to play happy families, are we? Do you think you can trust me that far?' she derided, and he smiled grimly.

'I trust you to know what side your bread is buttered on,' he remarked, and Tasha saw red.

'Damn you! How many times do I have to tell you I don't want your money? I just want you!' she choked out despairingly. The set look on his face told her that she was wasting her time. 'Oh, what's the use?' Tired and defeated, Tasha turned around and began to remount the stairs.

'Tasha?' Chase called after her, making her pause and look down over the banister.

'I'm tired, Chase,' she said flatly. A tiredness which was not entirely due to lack of sleep. She was heartsick and weary.

'I won't keep you. I only wanted to know if you'd bought a gift for Evan.'

She shook her head. 'No. Shall I get something tomorrow, or would you rather do it yourself?'

'You do it. I trust your judgement.'

He said it so easily, as if he'd never had a moment's doubt. How she wished he could trust in her love for him that unquestioningly. 'Very well.' She continued up to her room, shutting the door and dropping onto the bed, to stare blankly up at the ceiling.

She wished that she could cry, but the pain she felt had gone too deep for that. The future looked so bleak. Chase was never going to admit that he still loved her. She had forfeited that when she'd lost his trust. She had decided to stay because she'd hoped to regain that trust, and that he would come to forgive her. But what if he never did?

It was a terrifying thought which stayed with her all the next day as she shopped for a gift and drove up to the Calders' home in Maine.

John and Elaine owned a large house on the lake shore. It had been their summer home, but since John had retired from actively practising law the Calders had moved out of the city permanently. Tasha had been there several times during the months of her marriage to Chase, but this was the first time she had ever arrived alone.

They came out to greet her with affectionate hugs, but were clearly perplexed not to see their son.

'He had to stay in town to see a witness tomorrow,' Tasha explained quickly, but Elaine was not to be easily swayed from her disapproval.

'You've never driven all that way on your own in your condition?' his mother exclaimed. 'What was Chase thinking of?'

'I didn't mind, really,' she lied. She had minded; she just hadn't had a choice.

'Well, I must say I'm surprised at him! It won't do, and I shall tell him so. You must be absolutely exhausted. Come along inside and I'll get you a nice hot cup of tea.'

Tasha found herself cosseted and fed and was filled with a strong desire to confide in her mother-in-law, but Chase didn't want his family to know that anything was wrong so that recourse was denied her. She couldn't ever remember feeling so helpless or so in need of good advice, yet unable to get it.

It wasn't until she went up to the room they always used that she discovered something that she felt sure Chase had forgotten. The bed. He hadn't shared her bed since Natalya's visit but, whereas sleeping in the guest room was possible at home, he couldn't get away with that here.

The thought filled her with mingled apprehension and eagerness. In bed, he had never been able to hide his feelings from her. Could that be why he had moved out—because he couldn't trust himself to keep the physical distance his mind demanded? It hadn't occurred to her before, but now she gave it serious thought.

Had she found a chink to break the wall he had built between them? To use sex against him wasn't how she wanted to win him back, but it could just be the way. If she could only once get him into bed with her, who knew what might happen? It was an opportunity she couldn't afford to ignore.

That night she slept dreamlessly, awaking to a bright, sunny day full of promise. There was plenty to do to keep her occupied, but as the day wore on she kept glancing at her watch with increasing frequency. Chase didn't arrive, and she was actually beginning to wonder if something had happened to him when he rang. Tasha was talking to Elaine when the housekeeper called her to the phone.

'The meeting's been put back. I'll be later than I expected,' he said shortly, and Tasha could hear voices in the background.

Disappointment surged through her—for Evan and for herself. 'But you are still going to make it, aren't you?' she queried, miming a shrug to Elaine who had come to stand by her.

'You sound disappointed,' Chase's voice echoed hollowly down the line, losing none of its mockery with distance.

Tasha sighed wistfully. 'I am. I miss you,' she confessed huskily, and for a moment she thought that silence was to be her only answer.

'Is my mother there?' he asked, making her frown.

'Yes, do you want to speak to her?'

'No. I just thought that might explain why you were being so affectionate,' Chase responded sneeringly, and Tasha caught a pained breath.

With his mother standing there, she couldn't protest the way she wanted to. 'I meant it,' she was forced to say lamely, knowing that it did little good.

'I'll be there as soon as I can. Apologise to Mom and Evan for me.' With that he hung up, leaving her staring unhappily at the receiver.

'Is anything wrong, dear?' Elaine asked, and Tasha hastily set the phone down and produced a rueful smile.

'That was Chase. He's going to be late, I'm afraid.'

His mother looked crestfallen. 'That's too bad but, after a lifetime married to a lawyer, I can't say I'm surprised. Disappointed, but not surprised. Come along, let's cheer ourselves up with a cup of coffee.'

Tasha allowed herself to be led away, but she found it hard to relax. As the afternoon drifted into evening other members of the family turned up by the carload, but not even they proved a lasting distraction. It took a determined effort to throw herself into the party atmosphere, and after a couple of hours she had to excuse herself and seek a moment's peace.

The library was an oasis of calm yet she found herself drawn to the window, watching for the sweep of headlights on the drive. If only Chase would come. It had been hours since his call. Surely no meeting could take that long?

Footsteps sounded behind her, and she turned to find Chase's younger brother, Evan, smiling as he advanced on her. 'So this is where you've got to.' Joining her, he took a quick glance out of the window. 'No sign of Chase yet?' He sounded offhand, but Tasha knew that he was disappointed that his brother hadn't yet arrived.

'I'm beginning to think we'll see the second coming before we see him!' she said caustically, and Evan grinned.

'To hell with it. Forget Chase and come dance with me,' he said, and Tasha had to smile back at his boyishly handsome face.

'OK, so long as Isobel doesn't mind,' she agreed, taking his arm and accompanying him back to the patio.

'Oh, don't worry about Isobel.' He casually dismissed his brand new fiancée. 'She sent me to find you. She thought you looked a bit lonely.'

Tasha wondered if her face was an open book for everyone to read. 'I'm about to go from lonely to angry,' she pronounced wryly, and he chuckled.

'That's the way. I like the idea that Chase's life won't be worth living if he doesn't turn up soon,' he said with relish.

'I'm sorry Chase isn't here, Evan,' she apologised as they began to circle the small dance floor.

'Don't worry about it,' he shrugged. 'I'll get my revenge, just you wait and see!'

She laughed as he'd intended her to, and let herself

drift with the music. After a couple of dances Tasha insisted that he went back to Isobel but he took her with him, and the three of them stood chatting at the edge of the crowd.

Tasha didn't know how many minutes had passed when she felt her senses stir in a way she knew so well. Chase was here. She'd always known when he walked into a room. It was as if her antennae picked up a positive charge of energy, which raised the fine hairs on her skin. Eagerly she began to scan the couples as they swirled around them, but it wasn't until a gap appeared that she found herself staring straight into his silvery grey eyes.

His gaze was so intense that she felt mesmerised and couldn't look away. Her heart lodged in her throat as something white hot and elemental shimmered in the air. It was recognition. The instinctive knowledge that the other person was a soul mate. That one being who made the other complete. Tasha experienced a burst of elation, for it was a reciprocal thing. Chase couldn't look at her like that unless he knew it too.

Seconds later he was gone as the dancers blocked him from her view, but she knew what she had seen. Hope rose like a faint but steadily burning candle in her heart. Maybe she would get back what she had lost.

'Chase is here,' she told Evan, and he stopped talking immediately.

'Where?' he asked, turning to scan the patio, but Tasha had already started to push through the crowd so he grabbed Isobel's arm and set off in pursuit.

Entering the less populated dining-room—which had been cleared to hold the bar and the tables of food—Tasha discovered Chase, talking to his parents. Her breath checked at the sight of him. He had been to their room because he was wearing the dinner suit she had

laid out for him. As she approached she saw his head
lift as he, like her, sensed the presence of the other.
Slowly he turned to face her.

'Chase.'

His name was a soft breath on her lips and, made
incautious by the way he had looked at her, Tasha went
to him as she always had—placing her hands on his
chest and tilting her head up for his kiss. Only then did
she see the chill in his eyes, and she knew that he was
going to fight what he felt. There was no pleasure for
him in knowing that they were made for each other. He
had hardened his heart, and it simply did not exist.

He saw her recognition of his resolve, and smiled
grimly. 'Tasha.'

Her name was a whisper, too, but it echoed in emp-
tiness, and she paled as he lowered his head and pressed
his lips to hers. It was a kiss which lasted a fraction of
a second, but its pain stretched on interminably. Careful
to hide her despair from him, Tasha lowered her lashes
as he released her again.

'Damn it, Chase, what took you so long?' Evan demanded to know from somewhere behind her, and Tasha
was gently but firmly put aside as Chase greeted his
brother.

'Did you think I'd miss your big night?' he teased
lightly, slapping his brother on the back. Tasha watched
with a sick heart, hating the jealousy which stabbed at
her when she saw the obvious affection between the two
brothers. It was unworthy, but she couldn't help it. She
hurt, and it didn't matter that it was her own fault. He
was breaking her heart.

'I would have been here sooner,' Chase was saying
easily, 'but unfortunately the interview took longer than
I expected, and then there was an accident on the high-
way. It looks like I missed a good party!'

Feeling trapped by the need to keep up the illusion of a perfect marriage, Tasha knew only one way to react and keep her pride. She came out fighting. Chase might want to deny what they shared, but she would not make it easy for him.

Knowing that he couldn't shake her off without arousing undue curiosity from his family, Tasha slipped her arm through his. 'And there was I thinking that you were deliberately trying to avoid me!' she teased, feeling just like the clown who laughed through his tears.

Chase grinned, though his eyes told her that he knew what she was doing and was furious. 'Now why would I do that, darling, when you know how I feel about you?' he countered softly, with the accuracy of a surgeon.

Though she knew she was no match for him, she refused to give up. Her chin went up a fraction. 'So you do still love me?' she provoked him, and watched anger flare in his eyes before he got it under control and met her blow for blow.

'Why don't you ask me that again later when we're alone and I can give it the attention it deserves?' he returned seductively and everyone laughed, including Tasha who alone knew he was being anything but loving.

She forged on, taking grim satisfaction from knowing that she was hitting back. 'Avoiding the issue, counsellor?' she challenged, and his eyes narrowed.

'Not at all. You know I love you as much as you love me,' he told her, and her lashes flickered at that palpable hit. He didn't believe that she loved him, which made his love for her absolute zero.

Yet it wasn't true, and she looked him right in the eye and told him so. 'It's nice to know you'd die for me, too, but relax. I won't ask it of you just yet!'

Before Chase could respond his father clapped a hand on his shoulder.

'I get the feeling we're superfluous,' John Calder observed drily. 'That being so, I intend to take my wife out to the patio and smooch with her. The rest of you can please yourselves!'

'Smooching sounds like a good idea, Dad. We'll join you,' Evan called after his departing parents. 'See you later, Chase...Tasha.'

The second they were on their own all pretence of harmony vanished. Chase removed his arm and turned to the hovering barman, ordering a Scotch and downing a healthy swig of it.

'Dutch courage, darling?' she couldn't help sniping, and he sent her a savage look.

'Getting rid of a nasty taste in my mouth.'

Stung, she flushed angrily. 'Was there really an accident?'

Chase eyed her mockingly. 'Why don't you ring the police? You'll probably accept their word before mine.'

'That could be because you've hardly spoken a dozen words to me lately,' Tasha returned pointedly.

Grey eyes narrowed on her pale face. 'I thought I was acting with admirable restraint,' he ground out harshly, emptying his glass and setting it aside.

'By not talking to me?' Tasha asked caustically, and Chase smiled thinly.

'By not choking the life out of you! Now, if you'll excuse me, I want to have a word with my cousin, Alex,' he said, and walked away from her.

Fighting a frustration that bordered on despair, Tasha watched his retreating back. He had closed his mind against her and wasn't going to give an inch. Her loneliness deepened. She missed their closeness. Not just the physical, but the closeness of mind and spirit. If she didn't get it back, if she was supposed to remain in the wilderness for ever, she didn't know if she could stand it.

Before she could decide what to do next one of Chase's cousins claimed her for a dance. David was tall, blond and good-looking, and deeply in love with a woman who didn't seem to know he was alive. He was also a charming flirt, and just what her bruised spirit needed.

'I hope Chase won't mind me borrowing his wife,' David remarked teasingly as they circled the floor, and Tasha's smile was wry.

'Of course not. He trusts you,' she replied. What she didn't say, and what kept the smile from her eyes, was that the only person here he didn't trust was his wife.

CHAPTER SEVEN

THE lake had a magical quality about it as it reflected the moon. Tasha found it soothing, restful, like the summerhouse which had been built close to the shore to catch the breeze off the water on sultry summer days. She had come here now that the party was over because she knew that she wouldn't sleep if she went to bed.

Eschewing the building, she stepped up onto the verandah and rested against the rail as she attempted to breathe in the peace inherent in the mesmerising lap of the water.

'Waiting for David?'

The unexpected question made her start and look round quickly. As her eyes grew used to the darkness of the interior of the summerhouse she picked out Chase, reclining on one of the wooden seats. She wondered how long he had been sitting out here in the dark.

'Well?' he prompted, and she remembered that he had asked her a question.

When she recalled what that question had been she frowned. 'Why on earth would you think I might be waiting for your cousin?'

'So you could continue your flirtation with him, unobserved,' he taunted, and her lips parted on a tiny gasp.

Flirtation? Of all the... She had danced with the man, that was all. Chase's reaction was out of proportion. Why, if she hadn't known better she would have thought that he was jealous! All of a sudden her heart went out of kilter. Perhaps she didn't know better. Could he be jealous? If he was, could she use it to get him back? All she knew for certain was that she had to test the incredible idea.

She licked her lips, her heart thundering in her ears. 'And if I was?' she probed coolly.

In one smooth movement Chase rose and came towards her, and she saw that since she had last seen him he had discarded his coat and loosened his tie. His shirt-sleeves were partly rolled up, too, making him look at once more relaxed and at the same time vastly increasing that sense of power he always carried with him.

'I would remind you that you are still married to me,' he said curtly, and the tension that crackled round him made her shiver.

Tasha's brain positively reeled at this act of staking his claim. Whatever he felt. Whatever he might, or might not, admit to he was not about to let her go! It was all she could do to keep her expression blank. He *was* jealous! Her heart started a crazy jig which made it hard for her to breathe steadily.

She knew that she had to feel her way with care because he clearly didn't know the message he was sending her. 'I know I'm married to you, Chase,' she said evenly.

His lips curled derisively. 'Do you? But it's not quite turned out the way you expected, has it? Perhaps you decided to flirt with David to spice things up a bit.'

Tasha caught her breath angrily. She did not deserve that jibe. She had done nothing to betray her vows. 'I was not flirting with David,' she denied vehemently. Jealous or not, he had no right to accuse her.

Chase's expression didn't change. 'I'm warning you—don't think you can play games with me, Tasha.'

Anger boiled up inside her. 'This is ridiculous! Why on earth would I flirt with David when everyone knows he's head over heels in love with another woman, and I'm madly in love with you?'

'You protest your love as if it were a talisman. But it's just words, Tasha, and we both know how well you manipulate them to get what you want. Lies drip off your tongue as sweetly and seductively as honey.'

Tasha balled her hands into fists in impotent rage. 'My love is not a lie. Everything I did was because I loved you and was desperately afraid of losing you.'

'A woman who loves a man would not do what you did, Tasha,' he said harshly, and she laughed despairingly.

'You're wrong. Oh, you are so wrong! A woman in love will do just about anything,' she argued huskily, knowing in her heart that she would never get through to him.

Just then a tiny gust of wind caught them, and a lock of Chase's hair whipped across his forehead. Instinctively Tasha reached up to brush it back. Her fingers glided over his cheek, the contact creating an electric tingle which forked across the flesh of her palm like a stroke of flame.

At the same time Chase raised his hand to do the same thing, and as their fingers collided she felt the warmth of his touch and heard the sudden hissing of air through his teeth as he breathed in sharply. His hand stilled and so did hers. Tasha found herself holding her breath as she stared into his grey gaze.

'Oh, Chase.' His name was just a whisper of breath as she waited for him to push her away again.

'Christ!' His exclamation was almost a tormented groan, and he briefly closed his eyes. When he opened them again his eyes held hers entrapped, and in a flash her pulse tripped into a faster beat. The air about them became still and thick.

Tasha forgot her anger. All she knew was that she had to convince him that he could trust her love.

'You know I love you,' she moaned brokenly and, because the night was so still, Chase had no difficulty hearing her.

'Why did you have to come out here?' he groaned.

'You call to me. Don't you know I'm nothing without you?' she sighed as her fingers began a gentle caress.

'Don't!' he ordered, pushing her away so abruptly that she stumbled and would have fallen had Chase not swiftly reached out and caught her, swinging her into his arms.

She fell against his chest with a tiny cry which became strangled in her throat as all the breath went from her and she drowned under a sensory overload. She felt Chase's chest rise as he abruptly took in air, and the bite of his fingers as his hands tightened on her arms. A trembling took hold of her and she raised her head, her eyes locking with his. It was all there for her to see. Everything he wanted to deny. This contact had shattered him as it had her, and tonight he had no defence against it.

'Tasha.'

Her name was a mere whisper from his lips, yet she heard him in every fibre of her being. It ended on a despairing groan. Time was suspended. She sensed the exact moment when will was overturned by need. His head began to descend towards hers, and he captured her lips with a hunger she met and matched.

Passion was instantly ignited as they both strained to be closer. Nothing mattered except the pleasure each could give the other. To Tasha it was like finding an oasis in the midst of a desert. He gave her life and joy and she couldn't get enough of him, nor give enough of herself in those blazing moments. Only the need for air eventually forced them apart to face each other, their eyes passion-glazed and their breathing ragged.

'Sweet heaven!' With a suddenness which was all the more shocking after those moments of passion Chase put her away from him, his expression changing to one of utter self-disgust. He turned away, his hands gripping the railing like grim death and his head dropping as he drew in much-needed air. 'What the hell am I doing?'

Tasha moistened lips bruised by his kisses. 'Making love to me,' she said poignantly.

That brought his head round. 'Love had nothing to do with it,' he gritted out angrily.

She winced inwardly, but had enough sense to know that Chase was angry at himself, not at her. Not yet. 'Whatever, you wanted me.'

A muscle flickered as he clenched his jaw. 'Yes.' The admission hissed through his teeth.

'I wanted you just as much, Chase.' Tasha confirmed what he had to know.

Chase stood up straight, thrusting his hands into his trouser pockets. 'You think that will make me despise myself less?' he threw at her savagely, driving a stake through her heart.

Dear Lord, it hurt as he had meant it to and Tasha felt the heat drain out of her blood, making her shiver though the night remained sultry. 'Damn you, Chase. Right now I wish I could hate you!' she forced out in a painfully tight voice, and turned away. She had to get away. She simply could not stay and let him vent his anger on her.

Unsteady legs put much-needed distance between them. He had a thousand ways to hurt her because she loved him. It would hurt less if she could hate him, but she still loved him. She knew in her soul that she always would, no matter what happened.

* * *

Tasha stirred with a heavy sigh. The bedroom was bathed in muted sunshine, enough to show her that the other half of the bed had remained empty all night. She didn't know where Chase had spent the night, and it didn't surprise her that he had managed to avoid sharing a room with her. Not after what he had said out by the lake.

It wasn't very nice to think that Chase despised himself for wanting her, but the one thing to come from her restless tossing, before sleep finally claimed her, was the knowledge that he did still want her. That sizzling attraction which lit up the air around them was still very much alive. He would fight it to the death, but he could no more deny it than she could. And if he could want her then he could still love her—somewhere deep inside.

He was angry with her. What she had done was wrong, and she would never deny it. But surely, surely, he would come to see that what they had was special? Too special to throw away. Then he just might allow himself to love her again. Freely, without regret.

Unwilling to lie there with her thoughts, Tasha sat up without thinking and a wave of nausea caught her. Thrusting back the covers, she ran to the bathroom. When the spasm was over she splashed cold water on her face and brushed her teeth. Feeling marginally better, she showered, then slipped into crisp white jeans and an emerald T-shirt. A flick of the brush through her hair and she was ready to join the family downstairs.

Stillness was what struck her as she crossed the hall. The whole house appeared silent. The lounge was empty, she discovered when she poked her head round the door. Feeling rather like the last person in the world, she went in search of a cup of tea.

The sunny breakfast room was situated at the back of the house, overlooking the lawns and the lake. The table was laid, and there were signs that it had been used but, apart from that, the room was empty. Turning to the sideboard, she found a fresh pot of tea on a warmer— which meant that somebody was about. With a faint smile she decided, first come, first served, but even as she reached for the pot it was as if there was a shift in the atmosphere and she experienced a prickling sensation over her whole body as if every single hair had stood to attention.

Tasha slowly turned round. Chase stood in the doorway leading to the kitchen, looking as if he had been poured into leg-hugging jeans and a plaid shirt. Ordinarily she would have simply walked into his arms, but now she had to resist it. Tearing her gaze away, she dragged in air as she turned back to the table and reached for the teapot.

'Tea?' she asked, clearing her throat and willing herself to act normally. But it wasn't easy when she sensed him coming closer, and her hand began to shake quite badly so that she could barely pour the liquid into the cup.

One large hand reached out, closing over hers and steadying the pot. 'You'll scald yourself if you're not careful,' Chase said gruffly, his voice thickening as he, like she, was made sharply aware of the heat their touch generated.

Tasha felt her legs go weak, as they always did, and closed her eyes as he took the pot from her and set it down. She longed for things to be as they had been so that he would turn to her and take her in his arms. She fancied that she could already feel the brush of his lips, the....

Footsteps echoed down the hallway, getting closer by the second. Her eyes shot open, and she turned to face the door as Evan swept into the room. He caught sight of his brother with his hand still on the teapot and shot him a hopeful grin.

'Oh, good, tea. Pour one for me, will you, Chase?' he urged cheerfully, taking a seat at the table and eyeing each of them in turn. 'Morning, Tasha,' he said blithely. 'You look tired. In fact, you both do. What have you been up to?' he chortled, with less than sly innuendo.

Tasha found it impossible to resist Evan's boyish charm. 'I don't know about Chase, but you can put my tiredness down to morning sickness,' she confessed truthfully, and heard Chase curse under his breath.

'Sit down, Tasha,' he ordered immediately, studying her profile himself, and his mouth tightened at the evidence. 'I'll bring you a cup of tea. Do you want anything to eat?'

His concern closed around her like a protective cloak, and the smile she sent him was free of strain. 'Dry toast usually helps,' she told him, and took the seat Evan had jumped up to pull out for her.

'I'll get Maudie to make some,' Chase said brusquely, setting a cup of tea before her then disappearing into the kitchen to speak to the housekeeper.

'Miserable beggar, isn't he?' Evan complained. 'Anyone would think he'd had no hand in getting you pregnant in the first place!' he added, rising to get his own cup of tea before rejoining her.

At least she could be thankful that Chase had had no doubts about being the father of her baby. If he had she didn't know what she would have done. 'He's angry at himself for forgetting I might be unwell,' she told Evan, knowing that was the reason for Chase's gruff behaviour. He might be angry with her, but he wouldn't knowingly hurt her by ignoring the difficulties of her condition. It was a significant contradiction which she doubted if he saw himself. But she did, and it strengthened the hope inside her.

Beside her, Evan skewed sideways to study her. 'I must say, pregnancy seems to agree with you—discounting the sickness, that is. You're positively blooming.'

Tasha laughed, smoothing her still-flat stomach. 'I think it's a bit too soon for that to fit,' she demurred.

'What's too soon?' Chase asked, coming in with a rack of toast which he set before her. He hooked out a chair opposite and sat down.

'Tasha doesn't think she's blooming, but I do. There's just something about her... Like Ali, you know.' He referred to his sister, who was expecting her baby any time now. 'What do you think, Chase?' Evan looked to his brother for support.

Tasha found herself holding her breath as she stared at her husband. What would he say? Would he be honest or lie, and would she know the difference?

Chase took a long time to reply. Slowly his eyes drifted from his brother to Tasha. 'I think she's even more beautiful than she was before,' he declared thickly, and her eyes locked with his helplessly.

'Do you mean that?' she asked huskily, hearing her heart thumping in her chest.

'I wouldn't lie to you, Tasha,' he said levelly, and took all the joy out of her. She paled. How could he have said that? To give with one hand and take with the other was too cruel!

Uncharacteristically graceless, Tasha pushed herself to her feet. 'Excuse me,' she muttered. Biting back an emotional surge of tears, she hurried from the room.

Chase caught up with her in the hallway, catching her arm to halt her flight. 'Wait! Damn it, wait, will you?' He overcame her struggles to break free with an effort.

'I'm sorry. I didn't mean it that way,' he apologised, and Tasha turned eyes filled with hurt on him.

'Is there another way?'

He sighed, releasing her to rub a hand around his neck. 'I only meant to say that I was telling the truth. It wasn't intended as a put-down.'

Tasha folded her arms protectively around herself. 'Only because you didn't happen to think of it!' she said tightly.

Chase's teeth snapped together audibly. 'Damn it. I'm trying to apologise!'

'And is that supposed to make it right? Because you've said you're sorry?' She threw his own words back at him intentionally, and his head went back as it registered.

'It's hardly the same thing. I never meant to hurt you.'

Her eyes were awash. 'And I never meant to hurt you, either. Only you don't believe me, so why should I believe you?'

Chase glared at her for several seething seconds, then spun on his heel and strode back into the breakfast room. Tasha averted her head, blinking back the tears she didn't want to cry. She wanted to be angry, not emotional, and cursed her condition for causing the edges to blur. When she was in control again she wandered through the house and out onto the patio. It had been cleared of party debris, and Tasha sank tiredly into a chair.

Not two minutes later a plate of toast and her cup of tea were set down on the table beside her. She glanced up automatically—into Chase's set face.

'Eat your breakfast,' he ordered, putting her back up at once.

'I'm not hungry,' she refused bluntly, which only made his expression grimmer.

'Eat it, Tasha. For your own good and the baby's. Don't cut off your nose to spite me.'

He was right, and she knew it. She didn't want to be sick, nor did she want to harm her baby. Grudgingly she reached for a piece of toast and bit into it. After watching her for a moment or two, Chase made himself comfortable on the patio wall. He ignored her, staring intently at the view.

He looked like nothing so much as a dog on guard, and her sense of humour surfaced as she realised that he wasn't about to leave until she had cleared her plate. With a tiny sigh she relaxed into her seat.

'It's very quiet. Where is everybody?' she asked after a while.

Chase turned his head to look at her, taking in the diminishing pile of toast with satisfaction. 'Mom received a phone call first thing this morning,' he explained, and Tasha's eyes widened.

'Ali had the baby?'

'A boy,' Chase confirmed, glancing at his watch. 'Mom and Dad left a couple of hours ago now so they should arrive soon.'

Tasha grinned. 'Was she coherent?' she teased, and Chase smiled ruefully.

'Barely,' he admitted, and they shared a look of amusement.

'Poor John,' she said with a giggle, and Chase's grey eyes danced with answering laughter.

'Dad was nearly as bad. I hope they don't have an accident.'

'Perhaps we ought to invite them to stay with us when the baby's due, then we won't have to worry about them,' Tasha suggested, and their eyes locked as a sense of togetherness settled over them.

Then a bird squawked in the tree closest to them and

the moment was lost. Made aware that his guard had dropped, Chase sat up straighter. 'We can worry about that when the time comes,' he said abruptly, and to Tasha it was as if the sun had gone in.

It had felt so good to talk with Chase as if nothing bad lay between them that Tasha wanted to scream in frustration. Instead she reached for her cup, using the time it took to drain it to compose herself. 'You're right. You were right about the food too. I was hungry.'

Chase stood and gathered up the dirty crockery. 'The last thing you need to do is make yourself ill.'

'No, Doctor,' she retorted mockingly, and he gave her a sharp look.

'I mean it, Tasha,' he insisted, and suddenly she knew why. He didn't trust her with anything...or anyone.

'Don't worry, I have no intention of harming the baby,' she told him coldly, and he took a deep breath.

'What is that supposed to mean?'

Tasha looked at him bitterly. 'It means that I know you don't trust me, but I would never deliberately hurt our child!'

Chase's jaw clenched, a sure sign of his anger. 'Believe it or not, I never thought you would. I was actually thinking of you,' he returned savagely, and Tasha realised that she had jumped to conclusions.

'If I misunderstood I'm sorry,' she apologised stiffly, and Chase sighed heavily.

'Forget it.' About to walk away, he halted and glanced down at her averted face. 'Evan and I are going to go fishing. Will you be OK while we're gone?'

She glanced up, trying to read his expression but failing. Would he stay if she asked him? She decided it was better not to put it to the test. 'I'll be fine. You go and enjoy yourself.'

After a long moment Chase nodded. 'If you need anything ask Maudie. We'll be back around dinnertime. Take care of yourself.'

Left to her own devices, Tasha spent the day lounging in the shade—reading or dozing. It was good not to think, and she allowed the warmth to push her cares to the back of her mind. Maudie, obviously primed by Chase, made sure she ate at lunchtime and supplied cooling drinks through the long hot afternoon.

By the time she went indoors to take a leisurely bath and dress for dinner she felt more relaxed than she had been for many a day. The feeling lasted until Evan knocked on her bedroom door.

Tasha smiled at his dishevelled appearance. 'You look like you had a good day.'

'Yeah, it was great. We stopped by the bar in town on the way home, and Chase ran into Simeon Harker. He's an old friend. Anyway, the long and the short of it is that Chase knew I was coming home to get ready to see Isobel so he told me to tell you he's having dinner with him. He said he knew you'd understand.'

With a flash of insight which could suddenly strike a person, Tasha suddenly understood very well. Chase was still avoiding her, but it was a different kind of avoidance. If he hadn't kissed her yesterday she might have gone on thinking as she had since he had learned the truth. She knew better now. He didn't want to spend more time with her than he had to. With his parents gone and his brother out for the evening, there would only be the two of them. They would have had to spend hours together and anything might have happened. He wouldn't risk it. She had him on the run!

'I see. Thanks for telling me, Evan. Give Isobel my love,' she said with creditable calm, and he went off, whistling, to shower and change for his date.

Tasha closed the bedroom door and leant back against

it, a hand pressed to her racing heart. She knew that she was right. How that soothed her aching heart and bruised spirit. Having spent days being constantly tossed on an emotional sea of storms—one second soaring with hope, the next plunging in despair—it was a relief to know that she was getting through to him. That all was not lost. He might avoid her tonight, but he couldn't avoid her for ever.

That evening she really didn't mind dining alone because her confidence had taken a boost. Afterwards she spent a couple of hours watching a play on the television and, when Chase still hadn't returned by the time it finished, retired early.

Sleep proved a stranger, though, and the more she sought it the more elusive it became. She tossed and turned, knowing that only one thing would really settle her—the sound of Chase coming home. She had no idea what time it was when she gave up the struggle and decided that perhaps a warm drink would help.

Shrugging on the silky wrap that matched her nightdress, she tied the belt firmly around her waist before she slipped barefoot from her room and padded downstairs. Flicking on the kitchen light, she began to search for the ingredients she required. Ten minutes later she was sitting at the kitchen table, sipping a steaming mug of chocolate.

At the sound of the back door opening she glanced up quickly.

'You're up late tonight, Maudie,' Chase said tiredly before he turned and saw that it was not the housekeeper who occupied the kitchen but Tasha. He froze with his back to the door, taking in the sight of her in her silky robe with her hair mussed from her sleepless tossing and turning.

Neither moved.

Caught out by this unexpected meeting, Chase had no time to raise his defences. 'I thought you'd be in bed,' he remarked tautly, yet his eyes burned with a heat that licked at her even from that distance, turning them a deep stormy grey.

Tasha set her mug down, the knowledge that he didn't want to feel what he was feeling making her nerves leap. She knew that she was right. She hoped that she was because she was about to leave herself wide open to attack. 'Hoped I'd be, don't you mean?' she challenged mockingly.

Blue eyes locked with grey, forcing honesty. 'Hoped,' Chase conceded grudgingly, rubbing a hand round the back of his neck as if that could ease the tension between them. 'Damn you, why couldn't you have been in bed?'

'I couldn't sleep. I don't like sleeping alone any more,' she confessed simply, and saw something flash deep in his eyes as she clearly struck a nerve.

'For Christ's sake, why do you do that, Tasha? You leave yourself wide open to be hurt!' Chase took an unsteady breath, walking slowly forward. When he reached the sink beside her he stopped, resting back against it.

Tasha watched him, vividly aware of the way the muscles of his legs flexed as he shifted to a more comfortable position. 'I don't know how you can hurt me more than you have. The way you reject me kills me,' she declared truthfully.

He frowned hard. 'What would you have me do?'

'Love me,' she said raggedly, making him push himself upright in a flash.

'Hell, don't you have any pride?'

There was a time for pride, but this wasn't it. 'Apparently not. Pride won't keep me warm, or hold me close at night.'

His jaw clenched tightly at her words. 'I can't give you what you want.'

Tasha's eyes flashed. 'You mean you won't!'

'Drop it, Tasha.' Chase said warningly, but Tasha shook her head.

'I can't.' She had too much to lose. So much to gain.

His lips twisted bitterly. 'Then you're a fool.'

She stared up at him, launching her most powerful weapon. 'Whatever I am—you want me. You can feel it as much as I do. You want to make love to me!'

He laughed bleakly. 'I have a healthy libido, and sex was always good between us.'

Tasha winced at the bald statement, but refused to let it draw blood. 'Don't cheapen it. What we had was more than just good sex. I loved you, and you loved me, Chase.'

'Loved being the operative word.'

Their eyes locked in silent battle.

'You won't give an inch, will you?' she asked tautly, so aware of him—of his strength and solidity—that it was an effort not to reach out and touch him. It was madness, of course. If she tried he would brush her off. He was a determined man. He couldn't trust her so he wouldn't love her. Emotionally or physically.

'I can't forget what you did,' Chase declared shortly.

Her lashes fluttered. 'And you won't forgive it, either, so where does that leave me? How long do we go on like this?'

'Until I can be sure,' he said firmly, and she shook her head despairingly.

'Until you can be sure of what? That you can trust me again? Tell me how to make you do that, and I'll do it! I'll swear on a stack of bibles, if that will help,' she invited, and the despair in her heart forced a wild sob from her throat. 'Hell, I'd go on national television if that was what it would take! Don't you know I'd do anything for you?'

It was instinctive for Chase to close the gap between them and reach out to take her shoulders, jerking her to her feet. 'I don't want you to do anything! I...' The words tailed away as he became aware of how closely he held her, and he shut his eyes abruptly while his fingers flexed on her bruised flesh.

There was an instant when Tasha felt him begin to pull her towards himself, and her heart leapt into her throat. Then, with a groan, he pushed her away, turning his back on her.

'Damn!'

She bit her lip, reaching out a tentative hand towards him. 'Chase...'

He swung round so fast that she jumped, her heart thumping at the look on his face. 'Don't touch me!' he grated out harshly.

Tasha hugged her arms around her body. 'Stop pushing me away.'

'I have to. Damn it, I have to,' he repeated, sounding more as if he was trying to convincing himself than her.

Her heart ached for both of them. 'Why must you, when we both know it isn't what you want?' she challenged brokenly.

To her amazement he laughed, albeit briefly. 'God, don't you ever give up?' he murmured, bringing colour to her cheeks.

'I won't give up on you. You'll have to kill me first.' It was no more, and no less, than the truth.

He stared down into her eyes and whatever he read there made him sigh. 'Do you have any idea how very much I want to kiss you?' he whispered, without a trace of pleasure at his need. Her lashes fluttered wildly.

'Yes,' she breathed back. She knew. Oh, how she knew because she felt it too.

As if it had a will of its own his hand left her shoulder, his fingers tracing the gentle curve of her cheek to finally brush across her lips. She caught her breath, feeling that touch like a brand. She saw the intent in his eyes, the mental struggle to do what he felt was right and then the movement of his throat as he swallowed, the need outweighing his resolve, and she brought her hands up to his chest to stay him.

'You'll hate yourself,' she reminded him, vitally aware that the instant her hands touched him they burned with his heat and tingled with the need to explore the flesh so tantalisingly close.

'I know,' he agreed softly, his head slowly lowering. Tasha felt her legs go weak. 'You'll blame me.'

'Probably, but I have to do this,' Chase groaned, and brought his mouth down to hers.

Right now she didn't care if he did blame her, for this was what she wanted. The brush of his lips over hers sent the world spinning away, and when his tongue stroked the sensitive flesh she was lost and opened to him with a sigh of pleasure.

She could not think, only feel. When his arms closed around her, pulling her tightly to his powerful chest, she groaned with delight. It felt so good. She shivered as his tongue sought hers, mating with it and taking her along a path she wanted to travel. Her hands slid up around his neck, her fingers tangling in his hair as they had longed to do.

As she had known it would be, one kiss was not enough. One quickly became two, three…and each was hungrier than the last, drawing a response which had them trembling in each other's arms and feeling the thudding of each other's hearts as the power of the passion they evoked threatened to become unleashed.

Then, as if from far away, she heard Chase curse, and the euphoric kisses stopped. Disorientated, she stared up at him, saw the passion die and be replaced with self-disgust. Though she had come to expect it, it tore her heart wide open.

'You were right. I shouldn't have done that,' Chase said bleakly. The grim set of his jaw was painful for her to see.

'Even if I say I'm not sorry you did?' she confessed with a faint smile.

He frowned at her. 'This won't work, Tasha.'

Tasha's heart thudded anxiously. 'What do you mean?' she asked uneasily.

Chase stepped back, putting some distance between them. Tasha instantly felt chilled. 'You can't win me over with your body, however delectable it is and however much I want to bury myself in it.'

A wave of colour rushed into her cheeks at his accurate comment. 'I wasn't doing that!' she protested faintly, but he gave her an unwavering look.

'Weren't you?'

Her throat tightened. Of course she was. It was the only weapon she had. She tipped her chin up. 'Do you blame me for trying?' she demanded, and Chase shook his head.

'I'd probably do the same.'

Easy for him to say, she thought, her lips twisting bitterly. 'Only you'd never get yourself into the situation I have, would you?' He didn't have to say anything—his grim expression was enough.

Suddenly her eyes were brim-full of tears. 'I can't win, can I?' She was going to lose him. The certainty of it was like lead in her heart.

Grey eyes narrowed on her distressed face. 'You shouldn't be getting upset like this,' he warned in concern, and Tasha gave a choked laugh.

'You have it in your power to make me the happiest woman on earth. All it would take is a few little words.' A tear escaped, tracking a line down her cheek. She swiped it away with the back of her hand.

'You're distraught.'

She wasn't getting through. She would never get through! 'I love you, damn you!' she choked out, meeting his eyes and finding the shutters were well and truly back in place. 'It doesn't help, though, does it?'

Chase's jaw tensed. 'No. It only makes it worse.' He turned away, his shoulders stiff with rejection. 'Go to bed, Tasha,' he advised as he let himself out of the house, without looking at her again.

Tasha stared at the closed door. Why on earth was she wasting her time? Nothing she said or did got her anywhere. She had lost him. Their marriage could go on for fifty years, but she would still have lost him. The huge gamble she had taken had been for nothing. She had believed that the risk was worth it but too late she had discovered that it wasn't. He would never forgive her.

CHAPTER EIGHT

TASHA watched Chase laugh at something his brother, Evan, said, and felt her chest tighten at the uninhibited sound. Today he was wearing jeans and a khaki bush shirt, which made him look breathtakingly attractive, and her heart gave a skip at the sight of him. She felt the sheer masculine impact of him deep inside. Nobody had ever affected her the way Chase did. Nobody else ever would.

She sighed, returning her attention to the dirty dishes in the sink. It was Maudie's afternoon off, and she and Isobel were clearing up after the lunch the four of them had shared.

'Tell me to mind my own business,' Isobel remarked as she reached for a plate and began to dry it, 'but do you want to talk about it?'

With a lurch of her heart, Tasha glanced at the other woman and met a sympathetic look which almost undid her. She had to drop her eyes and clear her throat to form a reply. 'I don't know what you mean,' she lied, and almost instantly felt a gentle touch on her arm.

'I know something's wrong, Tasha. Oh, it's not glaringly obvious,' she reassured Tasha at her aghast expression. 'Put it down to a woman's intuition. A woman in love's intuition. You're unhappy, and I'd like to help if I can.'

Tasha didn't respond immediately, but stared out of the window at the two men, who were playing ball on the lawn. She was tired of denying it. 'There's nothing you can do.'

Isobel's eyebrows met in a quick frown. 'But, surely...'

Tasha interrupted her with a twist of her lips. 'Believe me, this is something only Chase and I can work out. Though I would appreciate it if you said nothing to anyone else.'

'Of course not,' Isobel said quickly. 'Besides, Evan wouldn't even notice. I was beginning to think I'd have to pin flowers all over me to get him to notice me!' she added with a grin that made Tasha laugh.

'He can be a bit single-minded,' she conceded. Her gaze strayed outside again. It was something of a family trait, though Chase's mind tended towards stubbornness.

Her thoughts were interrupted by the sudden shrill ring of the telephone.

'I'll get it,' Isobel declared, crossing to the extension by the door. She listened for a second or two, then frowned and went to the back door. 'It's for you, Evan,' she called out, and both men began making their way back to the house. 'Charlie Hamilton,' she enlarged in response to Evan's questioning look, and he quickly reached for the receiver.

Tasha halted with her hands still in the dishwater. She had no idea who the caller was but, from the reaction of the other three, she knew that it was not simply a courtesy call. She knew that her instinct had been correct when Evan ended the call minutes later.

'A little boy has gone missing. He was camping out here with his family, and they thought he was asleep. It was a couple of hours before they noticed he was gone. They're getting search parties out, and Charlie wants us to help check the lake. Some of the boys have started out from this side. I said we'd cross over and work back towards them, Chase.'

'I'll get the walkie-talkies from the den,' Chase proposed, already heading towards the door. 'We can cover more ground if we split up.'

Isobel tossed down the dishtowel. 'I'll come with you. The more eyes the better.'

Tasha shook her hands free of suds and abandoned the sink. 'Give me a second to change my shoes and I'll join you,' she said decisively, and was instantly the target for three pairs of eyes.

Chase shook his head in blunt refusal. 'Oh, no, you don't. You'll stay right here.'

Taking exception to his tone, her chin lifted. 'Don't tell me what to do. I want to help, and I'm going with you.' He could shut her out of the rest of his life, but he couldn't stop her doing this.

Chase's jaw tensed. 'This is not a stroll. We're looking for a child, and we won't be able to look out for you!'

The suggestion that she was a liability had her hands balling into fists. 'I'm pregnant, not incapacitated. I certainly won't need your help, and I won't slow you down.'

'No, Tasha. I'm not going to waste any more time, standing here and arguing with you. I want you to stay here, and that's final,' he bit out coldly, and Tasha seethed with impotent anger. She had been wrong. She wasn't a liability—he just didn't want her with him!

She stood aside because her conscience demanded it but she wasn't finished, by any means. As the other three got themselves organised Tasha left the room and hurried upstairs. No doubt Chase would assume that she had given in, but he was in for a surprise. In her room she changed her shoes and waited until she heard the others leave the house, before running back downstairs.

Letting herself out of the back door, she headed off across the lawn and arrived at the dock in time to see their boat set off. She stepped down into the remaining runabout with grim determination. Nobody noticed her until she had started the engine and set out in pursuit, and then they turned at the sound.

A sense of unholy joy filled her when she saw Chase's thunderous expression, but she wasn't about to be intimidated. Nor could he turn around and make her go back. He was forced to allow her to follow them, but she knew that he would have something to say when they docked on the far side of the lake.

The others were waiting for her on the dock of a long-abandoned cabin when she eased in alongside. She could feel Chase's anger as she watched him tie off the boat with easy movements that flexed his muscles and simultaneously set her senses rioting. It annoyed her because she wanted to be angry with him, not attracted. When he straightened their eyes met, and she saw the flash of anger in the grey depths.

'What the hell are you playing at?' he demanded fiercely, helping her out of the boat with care despite the rage inside him. 'We don't have time for this.'

'Then don't waste time arguing with me. I'm here to help, and I'm staying.' She met his gaze head on. 'Be reasonable, Chase. Four of us have a better chance of finding the boy than three.'

'She's right, Chase,' Isobel backed her up, sending her a smile of understanding.

There was a moment's pregnant silence, during which grey eyes fought with blue—silently exchanging a message that she hadn't heard the last of this—before Chase answered.

'You'll go with me,' he stated curtly.

Evan sent Tasha a grin. 'Gracious to the last!' he declared, but she could see that there was more than a touch of confusion behind his smile. Maybe he wasn't as blind as Isobel thought.

Chase decided that they had wasted enough time. 'We'll go west; you two go east. If you find anything let us know, and we'll turn back. We'll do the same,' he declared shortly, and turned towards a barely perceptible trail which headed off westwards. With a wave to the others Tasha followed, and within minutes the two parties had lost sight of each other.

If it hadn't been for the tense silence and the urgency of their mission Tasha would have enjoyed the walk. It was a glorious day and the sunlight penetrated the trees, creating areas of sparkling light and dappled shade.

'I suppose you think you've been very clever, don't you?' Chase remarked after a while, causing Tasha to switch her attention from the lake shore to him. There was still a grim set to his jaw, and he was frowning too. She had an urge to reach up and smooth the lines away, yet she knew better than to touch him.

'Not at all. I simply wanted to help, and I couldn't see any valid reason for you to constantly refuse me,' she responded evenly.

Chase came to a halt with his hands on his hips, his eyes like gimlets as he observed her. 'You couldn't, huh?'

Tasha confronted him with her own chin raised. 'Not wanting my company doesn't rate as a valid excuse in these circumstances,' she charged pointedly.

A strange expression flitted across his face, and was gone before she could analyse it. 'I agree. I'd work with my worst enemy to save another life,' Chase remarked, stealing her thunder and leaving her gaping up at him.

She didn't understand. 'Then why...?'

Chase squinted up at the sky and heaved a sigh. 'Because you're sick most mornings, and at other times too, and you're hardly getting any sleep. This could be a rough day for someone in good condition,' he told her. 'Now if that offends you I'm sorry, but it's how I see it.'

Tasha bit her lip, realising that she had made a hasty assumption. He had been thinking of her and, because she had misjudged him, she had put herself in a position where she could be more of a hindrance than a help. All out of hurt pride. Damn.

She drew a ragged breath. 'I'll go back,' she sighed. They hadn't come far so she shouldn't have any trouble.

'No, you might as well stay now you're here.' Chase ruled that out instantly, much to her surprise and pleasure.

'OK,' she murmured, ignoring the fact that it wasn't the most gracious response, but he could so easily have allowed her to leave.

Having reached a form of understanding, they moved off again. Their eyes searched the undergrowth, even though they doubted that the child had got so far.

'You must be tired too,' Tasha observed. Chase didn't look as if he was getting much rest either. 'Where are you sleeping?' For a moment she thought he was going to refuse to answer, but then he shrugged.

'In the summerhouse.'

She had supposed as much. 'Those slatted chairs can't be comfortable.'

Chase groaned feelingly. 'They're not. I've got bruises you wouldn't believe. You should see my backside,' he added ruefully, making her laugh, and all of a sudden there was a shift in the air about them as their gazes became locked once more—only this time not in anything remotely resembling anger.

'I'd like to have the opportunity,' she said unsteadily, vitally aware that only a few feet of ground separated them and that it would be awfully easy to cross them. Yet she dared not. She had been rejected too often. He had to make the first move—if there was to be one.

That dangerous glint, which she had liked so much and which had been long absent, entered his eyes. 'Would you make it all better?' he flirted suggestively, causing the muscles of her stomach to clench wildly.

'Oh, yes,' she said huskily, and held her breath. She knew she could make everything better, if only he would let her. If only he would trust her enough to let her try.

Even as she thought it she saw the glint fade, to be replaced by doubt. For a moment Chase had forgotten but now memory was back, saddening her. Dulling the brightness of the day.

'Shouldn't we get on?' she suggested tautly, turning her back on him.

For a moment he said nothing, then she heard him move. 'You're right,' Chase agreed abruptly, and Tasha knew that his face would be etched into grim lines as he took that mental step back.

She chanced a look. The barriers were once more in place as he indicated the path he wanted them to take, making sure not to touch her—even by accident—as he took the lead. For half an hour they pressed on with barely a word spoken, the going getting increasingly harder as they approached one of the river valleys which fed the small lake.

Chase called a halt. 'We'll have to go inland a short way to cross the river. It shouldn't be difficult at this time of year. There should only be a trickle of water.'

Tasha sank onto a convenient fallen tree. 'Surely the boy won't have got this far?'

'I wouldn't have thought so, but kids can often surprise you,' he remarked then, catching a glimpse of Tasha's horrified expression, quickly smiled. 'Don't

worry, they'll probably find him curled up asleep somewhere and this will have been all for nothing. Charlie's
just covering all the bases by sending us out here.'

'The boy's poor parents must be frantic with worry.'
She could appreciate how they felt, and automatically
her hand went protectively to her waist.

'Right now, they'd give anything to have him back,'
Chase agreed. 'When they get him relief will make them
cry all over him. Then they'll want to kill the little darling for putting them through hell,' he added wryly,
making her laugh—which was what he had intended.

'I suppose you're speaking from experience?' she
teased, imagining that he must have been a tearaway.
That glint in his eye spoke of many adventures.

Chase laughed. 'I guess I gave my parents their fair
share of grief. Especially when we came here for the
summer.'

'You must know the area very well.'

His smile was reminiscent and roguish. 'I spent my
summers roaming the woods, the lake and the surrounding valleys. This is one of the easy routes. Some of the
trails I blazed would have turned Mom's hair white.'

Her eyes danced. 'You never told her?'

'Would you?' he challenged with a knowing look. 'I
would have been grounded, and no way was that about
to happen!'

'And there was I, thinking you never did anything
wrong!' she exclaimed with a chuckle.

Chase gave an offhand shrug. 'I've had my moments.'

'Haven't we all?' she responded, and at the same instant both of them remembered the most recent instance
when she had pretended to be her sister. An uncomfortable silence fell, and into it came the squawk of the
walkie-talkie.

Chase answered, and Tasha held her breath as she

waited to hear the outcome. When he signed off she raised her eyebrows inquiringly.

'They've found him. Apparently he'd made it as far as Riley's barn, then fallen asleep. They're taking him back to his family even as we speak,' he reported, and the relief on his face mirrored hers. 'I'll just tell Evan the good news.'

Tasha hadn't realised how tense she was until then. Now the tension seeped out of her, leaving her feeling weak and shaky, and she turned her face skywards to watch the play of the sun through the leafy canopy. It was so peaceful here that she could quite easily lie down and fall asleep.

'They're heading back.'

Chase's voice interrupted her musing, and she sat up reluctantly. 'I suppose we should, too.'

Chase studied her as if he was debating something in his mind, then seemed to reach a decision. 'In a little while. Come with me.'

That he was inviting her company surprised her as much as anything else, and she rose to her feet without a thought of refusing. 'Where are we going?'

A faint smile hovered about his lips. 'You'll see,' was all he said as he led the way onwards.

Intrigued, Tasha followed. Less than ten minutes later they came out into a sunny glade. She could hear the sound of water, gurgling over rocks, and crossed the open space to look down into a small gully. Sunlight danced on the surface of the water, dazzling her. Tasha was instantly entranced.

'It's beautiful,' she said in a hushed tone, and Chase glanced over at her with a smile that made her heart skip a beat.

'I thought you'd appreciate it.'

Her heart contracted. Oh, yes, she appreciated it. And

more so, the message he seemed to be sending. This was a special place to him, and he didn't share it lightly. That he had chosen to share it with her filled her heart with sudden hope. Why else would he have brought her to this enchanted spot if he didn't see a future for them? It had to be a sign.

Turning, she sent him a broad smile. 'Thank you for bringing me here.'

Chase inclined his head. 'My pleasure,' he returned throatily, and their gazes locked with an intensity of emotion.

It couldn't be sustained for long and when, as if by mutual consent, both dragged their eyes away Tasha was left adrift, wishing that he would just cross the gap which separated them, take her in his arms and end this purgatory they had been living in. Weakly she sank to the grass, watching out of the corner of her eye as Chase propped himself against a tree. Crossing his arms over his chest, he watched the play of water on stones.

She was caught by the sombre cast to his half-turned head. He wasn't a happy man. This thing between them had destroyed his peace, just as it had hers. 'Penny for them,' she called out, inviting him to share with her as they had before.

His gaze jerked back to her. 'You'd be paying too much,' he declared wryly, and her lips curved into a smile.

'That's a matter of opinion,' she argued softly. She wanted to go to him, soothe him. Say it would be all right. But she could do none of those things until he was ready to accept it.

'How much would you pay?' Chase challenged curiously, and Tasha shrugged.

'No price would be too high. For instance, I'd give a fortune to know what you're thinking right now.'

'Even if they're bad thoughts?'

Chase's soft question sent a shock through her, even though she laughed. 'In that case, I know what they are. If they're bad then they must be about me,' she replied with an odd wistfulness that caused Chase to frown.

'Is that what you think?'

Tasha quirked a mocking eyebrow. 'Was I wrong?'

'Not entirely,' he agreed solemnly, shifting to a more comfortable position. 'You were part of my thoughts, but not all of them.'

'The better part of them, but not the good—right?' Tasha rejoined self-deprecatingly.

'Actually, I was thinking of how your face lights up when you laugh. Your eyes sparkle like sapphires,' he declared in a voice so gruff that her heart did a wild plunge, her breathing suddenly becoming restricted.

Her heart thudded in her chest as she stared at him. 'If you have to say things like that you'll compel me to tell you that your smile is downright sinful,' she declared breathlessly.

Chase came away from the tree, but he had taken no more than two steps towards her when he stopped and breathed in deeply. 'I'd want to hear it,' he responded thickly, and Tasha closed her eyes briefly.

'You know, if I didn't know better I'd think someone up there was having a joke at our expense,' she sighed, with a toss of her head heavenwards. 'A very unfunny joke.' She was painfully aware that the air thrummed around them.

'Just lately I've lost my sense of humour too,' Chase agreed sardonically. 'But, damn it, ignoring you is like trying to make rain fall upwards. Downright impossible!'

Her throat closed over as the exchange of words deepened. At last they were communicating, and she prayed that she wouldn't say the wrong thing and end it too soon. 'This has been like a nightmare we can't wake up from,' she declared with a grimace.

'Tell me about it,' he rejoined ironically, and when she glanced at him they shared a moment of wry empathy. With a sigh Chase dragged a weary hand round his neck, drawing her gaze to the tanned skin showing at the open neck of his shirt.

Silence fell between them, punctuated only by the noise of the stream and the birdsong. Both were very much aware of the electricity which charged the small space separating them. Chase took a deep breath, flexing his shoulders to ease the tension there. Lord, Tasha thought as her stomach clenched, everything about him was so attractive. When he flexed his arms he made her want to be in them. When he smiled she longed to feel the brush of his lips on hers.

'Come on, let's go back,' Chase decided a moment later, closing the gap and holding out his hand to help her to her feet.

She took it, catching her breath at the tingling heat which shot up her arm at the contact. Determined not to throw herself at him again, Tasha made to turn away but, much to her surprise, with a deft tug on her wrist Chase pulled her back. She lost her footing, and an instant later found herself in his arms.

Her heart racing, Tasha clutched Chase's shirt as she found her cheek brushing the tantalising skin of his throat. She went absolutely still, while her senses began rioting. She could hear Chase's heart thundering in his chest, just as her own was doing, and every shaky breath she took drew in the scent of him. He was so overwhelmingly male, and every atom of her being responded to him. She burned with the imprint of his hands on her back, and her knees turned to jelly.

She knew that she ought to move away, but her

strength was gone. She could barely think of anything, except the way he made her feel. It was an ache which just grew and grew until she felt that she would die if he didn't kiss her. Her eyes drifted upwards, her nerves leaping as she witnessed the throbbing pulse in his neck. She couldn't take her gaze away from that revealing spot, and her lips tingled with a powerful urge to touch it—to reacquaint herself with the taste of him.

With a faint moan she gave in to the need which filled her, and her lips found the pulse unerringly. Above her head she heard Chase catch his breath, and felt the tell-tale increase in the rhythm her tongue now explored. Pressed so close to the lean male body, she could feel his arousal. A thrill of triumph coursed through her as she revelled in the fact that Chase wanted her. Wanted her so much that he wasn't fighting it, and she had the means to drive him out of control. That knowledge stole the remaining strength from her legs.

Chase caught her as she sagged against him. With a groan, he snagged his hand in her hair and tipped her head backwards until he could gaze down into her heated face. She saw the battle going on in him, and the moment when he gave up the struggle. His hand moved to cup her cheek, his thumb gently stroking her lower lip.

'Dear God, Tasha, I want you so damned much!' he declared gruffly, and brought his mouth down on hers.

As she kissed him back Tasha prayed that this time he would not stop. That this time he would love her and realise that this was how it had always been meant to be.

CHAPTER NINE

IT WAS like plunging into an inferno. Desire was hot and remorseless. They had been apart too long, needed too much, to be gentle with each other. Passion would not be satisfied by one kiss but a single kiss could, and did, ignite it. Chase plundered her mouth, bruising her lips, but Tasha welcomed the thrust of his tongue. She needed affirmation, and nothing mild would do.

Breaking the steamy kiss with a gasp, she flung her head back and shivered as Chase took up the invitation to caress the arch of her throat with lips and tongue. She barely felt the brush of his fingers as he dealt with the buttons of her blouse, only the gentle breath of air as the material was pushed aside, baring her to his avid gaze. Chase captured her breast in his hand as if it were something precious, stroking it first with his thumb and then with his tongue as his mouth claimed her tumescent flesh.

She groaned aloud as the muscles in her stomach contracted, setting up a throbbing ache between her thighs. It was a sweet delirium. Painful but, oh, so necessary. And she wanted Chase to feel it too. With a cry Tasha freed her hands to tear at his shirt, pushing it aside impatiently until she could run her hands over the sensuous planes of his chest, searching for the flat male nipples. She heard him groan when she found them, then felt him shudder when she lowered her head to tease him with her tongue.

The time for retreat was long gone. Caught up in the fires of mutual passion, they sank to the grass and reached for each other in increasingly desperate caresses. Their clothes vanished, and there was only the tantalising glide of flesh on flesh. There was no part of her that he didn't kiss; no part of him that she didn't caress with her hands. When Chase settled between her thighs their sighs of satisfaction mingled in the sultry air of the glade. Yet nothing could compare with the intense emotion both experienced when he thrust into her, joining them once more.

He stilled, muscles straining for control, and looked down into her face in a kind of wonder and Tasha stared back at him, her eyes filled with all the love in her overflowing heart. This was where he was meant to be. This was the moment when everything was right.

Then he began to move. Slowly at first, drawing out the pleasure until it was almost pain, while the coiling tension grew ever higher and tighter inside her until Tasha thought it would be impossible to feel more. Yet there was. As Chase's control finally broke his thrusts became harder, deeper, shooting her out over the edge with a shattering cry which drew him after her.

She clung on, riding the waves of her climax and experiencing untold pleasure when Chase, too, found his release. He sank onto her with a shaken groan, and she closed her arms around him.

Peace descended on their tiny corner of paradise and, in the aftermath of their shared rapture, Tasha wondered, what now? Did what had happened mean that Chase was willing to put the past behind them and go on, or had it simply been the result of need and he would now regret giving in to his baser needs?

He stirred, lifting his head and meeting her eyes only fleetingly before glancing away. 'Sorry. I must be heavy,' he muttered, rolling off her and leaving her chilled inside and out.

Chase might not have looked at her for long, but it had been long enough for her to see the regret in his eyes. Something died inside her, and she knew it was hope. It was one blow too many, and she felt crushed by it. If making love with her couldn't break through the steel around his heart what could?

Nothing. Nothing ever could. Nothing ever would. She had been fooling herself. Living in a fool's paradise. But her eyes were open at last, and she saw everything as it really was. She had killed his love, and sex was a poor substitute when he clearly hated the desire he still had for her.

Feeling sick, she sat up and reached for her clothes—pulling them on with a kind of desperation. 'We should go back,' she said gruffly, struggling with the buttons which refused to go into buttonholes.

Chase had sat up too, and was watching her. 'Here, let me do that,' he growled softly, sending tingles up and down her spine. But as his hands reached for the cloth Tasha jerked away.

'Don't!'

His hands stilled. 'Why? What's wrong?' he challenged, his eyes on her averted head.

'Nothing. I just couldn't bear you to touch me right now,' she said thickly.

His expression grew stony. 'You don't want me to touch you, and you say nothing's wrong? Something seems pretty damn wrong to me!' he exclaimed, climbing to his feet and dragging on his jeans.

Tasha stood up. 'Why did you make love to me, Chase?' she asked abruptly, making him pause in the act of reaching for his shirt. He straightened and frowned at her.

A nerve throbbed in his jaw. 'Why do you think?' He

turned her question back on her and she crossed her arms about her waist, as if it would help to ward off the truth.

'Because you couldn't help yourself,' she stated bluntly, hoping that he would rush to deny it—but he didn't.

Chase took several steps away from her. Her eyes followed him, and she could see the tautness of his shoulders as he pushed his hands into the pockets of his jeans. 'No, I couldn't. I never could,' he confirmed expressionlessly.

She tore her eyes away from the broad back and long, muscular legs, wishing she could hate him. Wishing she could ignore him, but that was impossible when something inside her was tuned to notice the smallest move he made.

Her voice sounded rusty as she made herself speak. 'And now you regret it.' It wasn't a question.

Chase half-turned towards her. 'I have so many regrets I don't know where to start.' Squaring his shoulders, he faced her fully. 'We can't go on like this, Tasha,' he said tiredly, and her heart jolted.

Tasha couldn't help but look at him then, and it felt as if something had torn inside her to see the sadness in his eyes. Her own filled with tears which turned the glade into a shimmering, misty place. From somewhere she found the necessary strength to speak.

'Don't worry, you won't have to,' she declared brokenly and, spinning on her heel, darted towards the blurred shape of the path.

'Tasha, no!' Chase called after her, but she ignored him. She didn't want to listen to any more words. She just wanted to get back to the house where she could nurse her bruised spirit and decide what to do.

She ran on, following the twists and turns of the path but not recognising any of the trees and bushes her tears distorted. From a distance she heard Chase calling her, and then the sound of pursuit. It spurred her on, and she didn't see the root that tripped her up and sent her flying. She lay still for a moment, winded, but when she heard Chase not far away she staggered to her feet and hurried on.

'Tasha, stop! Not that way!' Chase shouted right behind her, startling her into swinging round.

It was an action which overbalanced her and she took two uncertain steps backwards, trying to recover. The third reached back into nothing and she teetered on the edge of the unknown, horror entering her eyes as she realised that there was nothing beneath her. Her eyes met Chase's, seeing the stark horror there, too, as he raced towards her. But he was too late. With a piercing cry she felt herself falling backwards.

'No!'

She heard Chase's stricken yell as she struck the ground, bumping and rolling down a steep slope which had been hidden by undergrowth. She scarcely felt the blows as they came one upon the other. Shock had turned her numb, but when she was tossed against something sharp and solid which broke her wild plunge she felt the pain and groaned.

Through the red haze which seemed to burn her whole body she heard scrabbling sounds, and knew that Chase was coming down to find her. Seconds later, in a shower of leaves and dust, he arrived at her side. He had managed to pull on his shoes, but his chest was still bare. There were cuts and scratches all over his skin, and all the colour had been leached from his face. He reached out for her, then stopped. She could see his hands trembling, and she knew that he was afraid to touch her in case she was badly hurt and he made it worse.

'Christ!' He dragged a hand through his hair, and

swallowed hard. 'What have you done to yourself? Have you broken anything? Where does it hurt?'

She hurt all over, but she didn't think she had broken any bones. 'My head hurts,' she said raggedly. She vaguely recalled it hitting something, and was surprised that she hadn't blacked out.

Chase swore quietly, but with a violence she had never heard before. With gentle fingers he probed her hair, seeking and finding the large swelling. 'You've got a goose egg all right,' he confirmed in a shaky voice. 'I'm just going to check you over. Tell me if anything hurts,' he ordered, and quickly set about running his hands over her arms and legs.

Sinking back onto his heels, he gritted his teeth. 'Nothing appears to be broken, but we need to get you to a hospital fast. I don't want to leave you here but the walkie-talkie is back there.' He nodded in the direction of the glade.

Tasha managed to smile faintly. 'I'll be OK. I promise I won't run off,' she added wryly, and saw pain flicker in his eyes.

Yet he took his cue from her, and smiled encouragingly. 'I promise I'll be right back.'

'I know you will. I trust you,' she replied simply and, if anything, Chase lost more colour.

He looked about to say something, then shook his head and got to his feet. 'Start counting, sweetheart. I'll be back before you reach a hundred,' he declared, and began the laborious climb back up the slope.

Tasha had only reached sixty when a sharp pain shot through her. Gasping, she moved her head and knocked the growing lump on her head. This time blackness welled up around her and she could do nothing but plunge into it.

* * *

Tasha stirred. She knew where she was from the faint but unmistakable scents of a hospital. She remembered floating in and out of consciousness. Remembered the pain, but now she felt free of it. She also felt empty, and she knew why.

She had lost the baby.

She knew it, though nobody had told her. Where there had been life there was nothing, and she felt...nothing. Nothing except a sense of inevitability. She hadn't been meant to have the baby, any more than she was meant to have Chase. Now everything was back as it had been, and he was free.

Her eyes slowly began a study of her surroundings. It was night, she realised, wondering idly what night. Had she been here one day or several? It hardly mattered. Nothing seemed to matter very much.

When her gaze fell on Chase, lying sprawled in a chair by the window fast asleep, she stopped. He didn't look comfortable, and would probably have a crick in his neck when he woke. There was the dark stubble of beard on his jaw, and he appeared to be wearing the same clothes as he had during their search for the missing boy.

Only one day, then. This must be Tuesday.

As if he felt the brush of her eyes Chase stirred, opening his eyes to blink blearily at her. When he realised that she was awake he sat up quickly, groaning and rubbing at his neck.

'Damn it, these chairs are torture instruments!' he complained, though his gaze was fixed firmly on Tasha, checking her out.

'You should have gone home to bed,' she told him tonelessly, and his eyes narrowed slightly.

'Not until I knew how you were,' he countered, rising stiffly and coming to sit on the edge of the bed.

Tasha shifted her legs out of the way. 'I'm fine, just a bit bruised.'

Chase hesitated, and seemed to find it difficult to find the right words. 'Tasha…' he began gruffly, and picked up her hand. She let it rest lifelessly in his.

'It's OK; you don't have to tell me. I know I lost the baby,' she said dispassionately, bringing a startled look into his grey eyes. They were red-rimmed, and she wondered vaguely if he had been crying. It hardly seemed possible, so she dismissed it as fanciful.

'The doctors say it was the shock. I'm sorry, Tasha. I really wanted that baby,' he said thickly, and she allowed her gaze to drift past him to the window.

'Did you?' she murmured flatly, and his fingers jerked closed around hers.

'Of course! How can you doubt it?' Chase raised his voice, and she looked at him.

'I'm sorry. I didn't mean to upset you,' Tasha declared unemotionally, and Chase stared at her as if he couldn't believe what he was hearing.

'What's wrong with you?' he asked sharply. 'You're acting as if you don't care when I know you wanted the baby too!'

Tasha pulled her hand away from his. 'Everything is much less complicated now,' she said by way of an answer, and Chase frowned heavily.

'Less complicated?' He echoed, shaking his head. 'This isn't like you. No way would you be so cold. It has to be the shock. Maybe you should talk to someone,' he suggested in concern.

She shrugged indifferently. 'You really should go home, Chase. It won't do you any good, making yourself ill.'

Chase stood abruptly, taking an angry step away before swinging round to face her again. 'Stop worrying about me, damn it! I'm not the one who went careering down a cliff! I thought you were dead!'

'Well, I'm not dead. I lost a baby, but that hardly makes me unique. It happens to hundreds of women every day,' she told him levelly, and anger—and something else—flashed in his eyes.

'And do they all take the news like you? Without a tear? Can you hear yourself? You could have been discussing the weather!' Chase exclaimed in disgust, his eyes glittering with something she knew couldn't be tears.

Tasha stared at him blankly. 'Why are you so angry? Can't you see it was for the best?'

He looked stunned by the suggestion. 'For the best? For whom?'

She frowned. Why couldn't he see it? It was so clear to her. 'For you, of course. You're free now.'

'Free?' Chase closed his eyes momentarily. 'Tasha, what are you talking about?' he asked in a rigidly controlled voice.

'You're free to get on with your own life.'

Chase didn't respond at once, but walked to the window and stood, staring out. When he did speak he didn't turn around. 'I see. That's very generous, but what about you?'

Tasha blinked in confusion. 'Me?'

He turned then, but the distance and low light made it impossible for her to see his face clearly. 'What are you going to do with your life?'

Her mind was blank. 'Oh, I'll think of something. But that's not important. I just want you to know you'll be free so you don't have to have any regrets,' she said firmly.

Chase took an audible breath. 'You think I won't have any regrets, now that I'm…free?' he queried softly.

Tasha sighed, feeling very, very tired. 'I know you won't. So, you see, it is for the best.'

'Do you think I don't love you, Tasha?' he asked, with the strangest inflection in his voice. It sent a quiver along her nerves, leaving them not quite numb any more.

'I know you don't want to,' she responded flatly. 'You regret it.'

Silence punctuated that statement, and it was a while before Chase broke it.

'Is that why you ran away from me? Because you think I regret everything, including the baby?' His voice sounded scratchy, as if it was hard to get the words out.

She sighed again. 'You're an honourable man, and it was a tie you wouldn't break,' she told him simply— because it *was* that simple in her mind.

'Oh, Tasha. I don't think I've behaved very honourably at all,' Chase pronounced wearily.

'It doesn't matter. Nothing matters now, does it?' It was a rhetorical question, and Chase didn't attempt to answer it. 'I'm tired. You really should go to bed, Chase. You're due in court tomorrow, or is it today? Anyway, you should get some sleep. You don't want to let anyone down.'

He laughed, an off-key sound that echoed round the room. 'But it's OK to let you down, isn't it?' he said bleakly.

Tasha frowned. 'You haven't. You couldn't.'

'Hellfire, woman! Don't say that!' he ordered shortly, then got a grip on his anger. 'This isn't the time to sort anything out. You're right. I do have to be in court on Wednesday, and it couldn't have happened at a worse time. I'll have to go, but I'll be back as soon as I can.'

'It's OK; I understand.'

'No, you don't,' Chase countered grimly. 'And I don't have time to put things right. Listen, sweetheart, my par-

ents are on their way, so you'll be staying with them.
At least I'll know you're being well looked after. Promise me you won't do anything hasty, Tasha,' he demanded huskily.

'All right,' she agreed. She didn't know what she was
going to do yet, but it wouldn't be a hasty decision—
just a logical one.

He looked at her hard and long as if he didn't know
whether to believe her, then he decided that he had to.
'We have to talk, Tasha,' he added firmly.

'Do we have anything to say?' she challenged. In her
mind they had already said everything.

A nerve fluttered in his jaw. 'More than you know.
God, I wish I didn't have to leave you here like this.'

'I know you have to go. I understand, and I'll be fine.
Don't worry about me,' Tasha reassured him, willing
him to go. 'I'm tired. I think I'll go to sleep now,' she
said flatly, closing her eyes and leaving Chase with no
option but to step away from the bed.

Yet he didn't leave immediately. He waited until her
even breathing told him that she was asleep, then he
went in search of a doctor.

When Tasha next woke it was morning. She felt battered
and bruised, but that blessed numbness still hung over
her like a shroud. Swinging her legs from the bed, she
was glad to feel no dizziness as she stood up and went
to use the bathroom. The mirror above the sink showed
her the superficial results of her fall. They would fade
in time, but the unseen ones wouldn't.

As she stared at her reflection Tasha knew that she
had to get away and think; had to go somewhere quiet
where she could make the decisions that had to be made.
The easiest one she had already made. To leave Chase.

She walked back into her room as the doctor entered from the corridor.

'Ah, up and about, I see. How are you feeling this morning? No pains, headaches or dizziness?' He allowed her to climb into bed, then did a quick examination.

'I feel OK,' she confirmed, wincing as his fingers gently probed the large lump on her head. 'When can I go home?'

'In a rush to leave us?' he queried drily, crossing his arms as he stepped back to observe her. 'You know, your husband is very worried about you, Mrs Calder.'

Tasha sank back against the pillows and stared out of the window. 'I know. I told him he didn't need to be.'

The doctor, a slightly balding man in his late thirties, raised an eyebrow. 'He thinks you're in shock after losing the baby. I'm inclined to agree.'

She turned her unflinching gaze on him. 'Because I didn't cry?'

He shrugged. 'It would be a normal reaction.'

'I don't feel like crying. Does that make me abnormal?'

The doctor shifted uncomfortably. 'No. Everyone reacts in their own way,' he conceded.

'Then I would like to leave. When can that be arranged?'

He glanced from her to the chart he was holding. 'Well, you're showing no signs of concussion. Providing nothing happens in the next twenty-four hours, I'd say you can leave tomorrow morning.'

'Thank you, Doctor, you're very kind.' It was a dismissal, and he knew it. Though it clearly galled him, he gave a shake of his head and left her.

Alone once more, Tasha closed her eyes. Tomorrow she would leave. All she had to do now was find somewhere to go.

By the time Elaine Calder arrived at the hospital later that day Tasha had got the name of a holiday resort up-state from one of the nurses, and had managed to book a cabin. All she needed now was her car and some clothes, and her plans would be complete.

She was mentally running over them when her mother-in-law came in. For the first time since the accident a lump of emotion blocked Tasha's throat as Elaine silently enveloped her in a hug.

'My poor, poor Tasha. What a terrible thing to happen,' she declared sadly, and Tasha felt the burn of tears behind her eyes.

'I should have been more careful,' she responded shakily as Elaine released her and sank onto the edge of the bed.

'Accidents happen. There can be no blame. It's sad, but there will be other babies.'

Tasha dropped her eyes. 'Perhaps.' She knew there wouldn't be, but couldn't say so.

Elaine reached out a hand and gently cupped her cheek. 'You say that now, but when the time is right...' Her shrug was eloquent. 'All you have to think of now is coming home with us.'

Tasha smiled faintly. 'You've always been very kind to me, Elaine.'

The older woman patted her hand. 'It's very easy to be kind to you, dear. You're a very lovely young woman. John and I both think Chase is so lucky to have you. Now, have they told you when you can leave?'

She stayed for an hour, chatting about this and that, and then left with a promise to return bright and early the following day.

Tasha was already dressed and waiting when Elaine arrived with John next morning. They drove her back to their home and, once there, she went up to the room she had shared with Chase, changed her clothes, packed her case and went downstairs again.

Placing her case by the front door, she went in search of her in-laws and found them in the lounge. She didn't go in, but stood in the doorway.

'I'm leaving now,' she said quietly, and the Calders' shock was evident as they turned to her.

'Leaving?' Elaine gasped. 'But where are you going?'

'I can't tell you. I need to get away, and I don't want Chase to follow me.' They were both on their feet now, facing her.

'Why don't you want Chase to find you?' his father asked, getting to the crux of the matter, and Tasha sighed.

'Because it's better this way.'

'Running away is never better, Tasha. Staying and sorting out the problem is the right thing to do,' John argued, but she shook her head.

'Not this time. The right thing to do is to put right what I did wrong in the beginning.'

Elaine's expression grew increasingly anxious. 'Tasha, dear, you're not making sense.'

'I've lied to you,' Tasha confessed bluntly, looking them squarely in the eyes. 'When I met you I let you believe that I was Chase's fiancée, but I wasn't. My sister and I are identical twins. She was the one Chase was engaged to.'

'Good heavens!' Elaine declared faintly, sitting down suddenly.

Doggedly Tasha went on. 'I fell in love with him, so I pretended to be her. Chase fell in love with me, thinking I was her.'

The Calders said nothing as what she said slowly sank in. It was John who rallied first.

'When did Chase find out?' he asked, and she knew that he at least suspected the truth.

'Only a week or so ago,' she returned gruffly, and Elaine gasped.

'Oh, Tasha, no!'

Dry tears scorched her eyes. 'So, you see, I have to go. It's the only way to put everything right.' She turned away but, after taking a step, she glanced back. They hadn't moved. 'Tell Chase he doesn't have to regret anything any more. He's free.'

With that she walked away, picking up her case as she passed through the front door. She tossed it into the trunk of the car, climbed in, started the engine and drove away, without once looking back.

Inside the house John Calder exchanged a meaningful look with his wife, then reached for the telephone.

CHAPTER TEN

DAYS later Tasha stood, leaning against the rail of the back porch of the cabin she had rented, and stared into the rain-swept night. She could barely see the river, and the hills behind were no more than a dark outline in the surrounding blackness. Idly she rubbed her hands up and down her arms to banish the chill.

She had been standing out here for hours. Long, empty hours. She had come this far, but no further. She had no idea what to do. A week ago leaving had been the thing uppermost in her mind. Now she had no purpose; no sense of urgency to do anything else.

Why rush when everything that meant anything was gone?

Her eyes probed the darkness for the thousandth time. It was probably beautiful here when the sun shone, but it had seemed to be raining ever since she left the Calders' house. She supposed that she ought to fix herself some supper but she didn't feel hungry. She didn't feel anything, except the chill of the wind which brought the rain.

She shivered.

'Cold, Tasha?' a gentle, instantly recognisable voice asked solicitously, and she glanced round.

Chase.

He was standing on the end of her porch, raking a hand through his rain-dampened black hair. Clad in a tan leather jacket, he had matching boots on his feet and faded blue jeans hugged his long, muscular legs.

'Shouldn't you be in court,' she said impassively,

thinking only that in order to have got here so soon he had to have left hours ago.

Chase took a step forward, spreading his hands. 'When my father rang me I got a continuance.'

After which he had come back, intent on finding her, and somewhere along the line the nurse had told him where she was. It must have been a simple matter after that to find her because she hadn't been hiding. But why had he come? She had made it so easy for him to let her go without a fuss. All he had had to do was do nothing. They both knew that he needed his freedom. He should have let her give it to him.

'I didn't hear you arrive,' she remarked dully, looking steadily into the grey eyes set in that chiselled, strikingly handsome face she would remember all her life. She studied her emotions dispassionately. She loved him. No other man could make her feel what this one did. She just shouldn't be with him. She knew that now.

'I walked up from the office. I didn't want to give you a chance to run again,' he informed her, never once taking his eyes off her. As if he did, indeed, think she would run.

It amused her. He ought to know better. 'There's a difference between running and leaving.'

'It amounts to the same thing,' he argued, and she supposed that in his mind it did because he couldn't see what she saw so clearly.

'So, you decided to come after me.'

'Did you seriously think I wouldn't?' he responded coolly, taking several paces forward and entering the light thrown from the window—which allowed her to see the tiredness around his eyes and the tight set of his jaw.

'It would have been better. You're only making this harder on yourself,' she said indifferently. 'You look exhausted, and you needn't have been if you'd done as I told you,' she added with detached exasperation.

'Thanks for the concern, but what makes you think it would have been easier to let you go?' Chase countered, moving to prop himself against the rail just feet away from her.

Tasha frowned at him. Why was he being so obtuse? 'Because you need to be free of me, Chase. You know you do,' she explained reasonably.

'If that were true why did I make you promise not to do anything hasty?' he argued smoothly.

Tasha sighed. This was so unnecessary. 'Because you felt responsible for me losing the baby,' she said unemotionally, and as her attention was distracted by the need to brush her hair out of her eyes she didn't notice how her reaction made his jaw tense.

'I am responsible,' Chase admitted, but Tasha shook her head.

'I was the one who ran.'

'But I was the one who made you run,' he countered, holding her eyes. 'Wasn't I?' he probed softly, and she shrugged.

'It hardly matters. The baby's gone. You're free.' Putting an end to something she now knew should never have begun.

It was her detachment that sparked his anger. In the blink of an eye Chase closed the space between them, grabbing her by the shoulders and swinging her to face him.

'Enough of this! I will never be free of you, Tasha. What's more, I don't ever want to be!' he declared passionately, his eyes blazing at her with a mixture of emotions—all of them fierce.

She ought to have been alarmed by his emotion, but she wasn't. It didn't even reach her. Nothing did any more. But she knew what made him act this way, and she wanted to ease his unnecessary guilt. 'You don't mean that,' she corrected evenly, and his fingers tightened painfully.

'Oh, yes, I do. I've never meant anything so much in my whole life,' he countered grittily, then swore when she simply stared back at him. 'Damn it, Tasha, you have to believe me!'

A sad smile curled at the corners of her mouth. 'Poor Chase, you have to stop worrying about me. I'm OK now. I'm not bothered any more by regrets.'

Chase closed his eyes. 'God, those regrets! You've no idea how they've returned to haunt me!' he said agonisedly, and the pain in his eyes was clear when he finally looked at her again. Slowly, reluctantly, he released her.

'You can't help how you feel. None of us can.' Tasha sought to ease his pain.

He looked as if he was about to say something violent, then restrained himself. 'I didn't mean it,' he said with forced patience. 'Not the way you think,' he added tightly.

Tasha shrugged. 'I don't think about it at all.'

'Well, you can think about it now!' Chase exploded, then swore and got a grip on himself. 'I'm sorry,' he apologised abruptly.

'It's OK,' she responded softly, and he had to glance up at the heavens for help.

When he looked at her the rigid control he had on himself was patent. 'No, it is not OK. I have to get through to you, Tasha.'

'I can hear you well enough.'

'With your head but not with your heart,' he contradicted tiredly. 'I want to explain.'

Tasha studied his pale cheeks and the slump of his

shoulders, and wanted to put an end to it. 'I really don't need explanations, Chase. They don't matter.'

His glance was razor-sharp. 'Well, they matter to me! I want... No, I *need* to explain. Will you listen?'

Tasha didn't want to. She knew that nothing he could say would change how she felt, yet he needed to talk. Perhaps if he did he would come to see things the way she did. 'OK, I'll listen,' she conceded, then shivered as a chill gust of wind caught her. 'I think we'd better go inside,' she suggested and, taking his acceptance for granted, led the way into the cabin.

It was functional, comfortably—if sparsely—furnished. The living area and the kitchen were at the front. Two doors led to the bedroom and bathroom. A handmade rug was spread before the stone fireplace where a fire lay ready in the grate, awaiting a match to set off the kindling. In a sort of half-circle around it were a rather battered couch and two chairs.

'You're soaked,' she exclaimed in concern, getting her first real look at him. 'Hang your coat on the rack by the door. You'd better light the fire. I'll get us something to drink.'

When she returned with two mugs of coffee, laced with brandy, the fire was blazing away and Chase was hunkered down in front of it, his hands stretched out to the warmth.

'Here,' she said, offering him a mug, and he stood up to take it.

'Thanks,' he murmured appreciatively, following her with his eyes as she sat in the corner of the couch. He didn't join her.

After sipping at her own coffee in silence Tasha finally looked up at him. 'I'm listening,' she prompted, and saw the tension stiffen his back once more.

For an age he simply stared down into his mug, but

then he sighed heavily and began. 'That day in the woods, after we had made love, you asked me if I had regrets and I said I regretted many things. I did, but making love to you was not one of them. I could never regret that,' he told her in a strained voice. 'When I realised what you thought I tried to explain, but you weren't listening. You ran, and when I saw where you were going I forgot all about explanations. My blood ran cold. I've never been so terrified.' He shuddered, dragging a hand over ashen cheeks.

'Then you fell and I nearly went crazy. But you were alive, and so brave. I hated to leave you, but I had to… And then you said you trusted me…' He looked at her, his eyes haunted. 'That's when I first began to realise what I had done. How I had let you down.'

Tasha frowned down into her own drink. She recalled him saying that before, but he had been wrong then and he was wrong now. He had never let her down. She was the one who had lied and deceived. 'You mustn't say that. You know it isn't true,' she said, and for the first time there was the faintest semblance of a waver in her voice.

Faint as it was, Chase caught it and his heart lurched at that first sign of emotion. Swallowing hard, he shook his head. 'God help me, it *is* the truth. I let you down by listening to my stupid pride instead of my heart.'

Her head came up at that, blue eyes searching his. Her conviction suffered a hairline crack. What was he saying? 'I don't understand,' she said uncertainly.

Chase took an unsteady breath before proceeding. 'When I found out how you'd deceived me I was angry,' he declared, and out of the blue a painful wave swept through her nerve endings, leaving them raw and exposed as she recalled that scene. She shuddered. It had been the worst day of her life.

'You were furious,' she agreed in a raw voice and tried to hold back the painful memories, but they refused to be denied. Dulled emotions suddenly became razor-sharp as feeling returned. She wanted to beg Chase to stop. She didn't want to go through all this. It hurt too much. But her voice seemed frozen in her throat.

Watching the play of emotions on her face, Chase winced and hated himself for the need to press on remorselessly. 'Standing here now, I can imagine how you felt. At the time all I knew was that the woman I had trusted implicitly was a liar.'

Tasha caught her breath as a violent trembling started way down deep inside her. She set her barely touched coffee down and folded her arms protectively around herself. 'I wanted to tell you but I was afraid.' She groaned out the words barely above a whisper, but Chase heard them and nodded grimly.

'And I proved you were right to be afraid, didn't I?' he declared in self-disgust.

The tremor increased, and it took all her strength not to let it show. 'You had every right to feel angry.'

'You had every right to expect that I would at least listen to your explanation and understand. It was a small thing when you consider that I never for one second stopped loving you,' he corrected bluntly, and Tasha closed her eyes.

'I love you, Tasha.'

That confession ripped away the remnants of the numbing cocoon which had protected her, opening a door in the depths of her heart and freeing the pain locked inside. It very nearly crippled her, and she doubled over with an agonised moan. All the emotions which had been shielded from her this past week returned with a vengeance. She remembered everything.

'You don't want to love me, though, do you?' she

charged achingly, her throat painfully tight with long-suppressed tears.

As pale as death, Chase set his mug on the shelf above the fire and sank to his knees before her. 'Look at me, Tasha,' he commanded gruffly, and she raised her head, her eyes tormented.

'Don't lie to me!' she snarled, and his lips twisted bitterly.

'Sweetheart, I don't intend to. I only hope you believe me. I do want to love you. For my sins, I thought I didn't but that was because I forgot what my heart knows about you. I did love you. I do love you. I just didn't want you to know it,' he revealed harshly.

Tasha stared into his eyes, seeking confirmation and getting it in the self-loathing she read there. She blinked as her brain kicked in. He hadn't wanted her to know. It hadn't been as she had believed—that he couldn't love her because he couldn't trust her. He had always loved her. He just hadn't wanted her to know it!

A blinding anger welled up in her, and her fist rose to crash against his shoulder. 'God damn you, why?'

Chase flinched from her anger, his hands balling into fists where they rested on his thighs. He knew that he deserved her anger. 'To punish you. But, as God is my witness, I didn't realise I was doing it until I faced the very real possibility of losing you. When I sat beside you in hospital I took a long hard look at what I had been doing, and I didn't like what I saw.'

Her chest was so tight that she felt it would explode with her anger and pain. 'And just what did you see, Chase?' she challenged achingly.

Chase gritted his teeth, determined not to hold anything back. 'I saw a man who hid behind the fact that his wife loved him too much to leave, saving him from having to tell her that he loved her. All the time I pushed you away with one hand I held onto you with the other. I refused you my love, while making sure I didn't lose you.'

Tasha slumped back against the cushions, staring at him. It was an unedifying tale, and as her anger slowly began to subside she could imagine what it must have cost him to tell the truth. For it was the truth. It was too painful to be anything else. It had stirred up her emotions and, like someone coming out of a long sleep, she suddenly knew why.

He had told her not just because she deserved to know but because he had seen it as the only way to stir her out of her apathy. He had told her knowing full well that it could blow up in his face. He didn't want to lose her, but he had put her needs before his own. That had taken courage.

'That's…quite a story,' she said huskily, wondering how two supposedly sane people could do to each other what they had done.

'You needed to know.'

Tasha sighed heavily. 'Now that you've told me what do you want of me?' she asked tiredly, and it was one of the very few times she had ever seen him unsure. Yet he pressed on.

'I want you to forgive me. I know I don't deserve it. Believe me, I'm not proud of the way I've behaved. I need you to forgive me, Tasha, as I should have forgiven you.'

Her laugh was brittle, full of the aftermath of pain. 'You don't ask for much, do you?'

'Is it too much?' he asked hoarsely, and sadness overwhelmed her.

Her eyes filled. 'I don't know,' she whispered brokenly. 'You hurt me so much. What I did was wrong, but I did it out of love. What you did…' Her throat closed up and she couldn't go on.

'You don't have to tell me,' Chase bit out for her. 'What I did killed our baby, and I'll never forgive myself for that!' he declared in a voice full to the brim with self-hatred. Abruptly he got to his feet and crossed to the window, staring out with a back so tense that it was painful to see.

'I don't know myself any more, Tasha,' he went on thickly. 'I didn't know I could be so selfish and cruel. How the hell can I ask you to forgive me? How can I expect you to keep on loving me when I can do what I did? I killed our child, for God's sake!'

Horrified, because she hadn't been accusing him of that at all, she watched his head bow down and recognised the unbearable weight of grief in the sag of his shoulders. Her own sorrow rose to choke her. He was taking all the blame, and she couldn't let that happen because it wasn't right. They had both made mistakes; done things they shouldn't have. It didn't make them unforgivable, just human.

'Chase?' She called his name in a voice choked by her own tears but, though he raised his head, he didn't turn round. 'I do forgive you.'

'How can you?'

'Because I love you,' she whispered brokenly and then he did turn, allowing her to see the tears in his own eyes.

Without hesitation she rose and went to him, slipping her arms around his waist and holding on tightly when he resisted.

'Don't, Tasha,' he pleaded brokenly, but she shook her head.

'I won't let go. I won't let you blame yourself. We both made mistakes. We were both at fault, and our baby…perhaps it wasn't meant to be…' she said broken-heartedly, and finally the tears she had been unable to cry began to fall.

With a groan Chase folded his arms around her, holding her crushingly tight as all the misery and grief poured out of her.

A long time passed before the room grew silent again. Tasha stood in the circle of Chase's arms and felt peace settle in her heart. She hoped that the tears that Chase had shed in her arms had eased his pain too.

Above her head he heaved a sigh. 'I didn't know anything could hurt so much. First the thought that I might lose you, then knowing that we had lost the baby. I cried that night, by your bed, in a way I hadn't done since I was a boy. I saw myself losing everything—all because of my pride.'

Tasha rubbed her cheek against the damp patch her tears had made on his shirt. 'Neither of us came out of this very well, Chase. Apportioning blame won't help. I think we ought to make a deal. We must both agree to forgive ourselves and each other for our mistakes,' she proposed, and Chase eased away enough to look down at her.

'Is it really going to be that easy?' he asked, searching her eyes for doubts.

She held his gaze. 'I don't want to fight you, Chase. I just want to love you.'

'I want that, too.'

'Well, then?' she prompted huskily.

A slow smile spread across his face. 'Here? Now?' he queried, and Tasha smiled back.

'Can you think of a better time and place?' she asked. They had hurt together and they had cried together. Now they had to begin the healing by loving together.

Chase brought his hands up to cup her face, his

thumbs gently caressing her tear-stained cheeks. 'Are you sure? I don't want to hurt you any more than I have.'

Her hands came up to cover his, and she turned her head just enough to be able to press a kiss to his palm. 'Do you love me, Chase?'

'More than life,' he responded huskily, and her eyes glowed with the strength of her own feelings.

'Then you won't hurt me. You could. You know you have, but you never will again. Not willingly. Not by choice. If I didn't believe that I couldn't love you the way I do. You've been my life since the moment I met you. I want us to be happy again, Chase.'

'We will be. That's a promise I'll spend my whole life keeping,' Chase vowed and took her lips in a kiss, the reverence of which stirred her to her soul. 'Come,' he said softly, taking her hand.

They lay down before the fire, and their loving was slow and gentle. Passion would come later. For now they needed to reaffirm the depth and breadth of their feelings for one another. It was, for Tasha, a rebirth. Their clothes were discarded and, with each caress of hands and lips, they worshipped each other, washing away the old memories and making new ones. A knowledge of their vulnerability made them careful of each other because what they shared was beyond price.

They rebuilt trust on strong foundations this time, and discovered a whole new realm of emotions. And when passion began to rise they did not plunge into the heady flood-waters, but held back and let it take them higher than they had ever been before. Only then did they become one, riding the storm and holding on tightly to each other as it broke over them. They drowned, died a little and emerged, cleansed and purified by the power of their love.

Much later Chase propped his head on his hand, the

other lazily stroking the velvet softness of her thigh. They lay spoon-fashion, facing the slowly fading fire.

'You realise we didn't use any protection,' he pointed out wryly, and Tasha captured his hand and brought it around her.

'It wasn't the main thing on my mind,' she said, sighing comfortably. 'I don't suppose anything will come of it.'

Chase ran a series of kisses along her shoulder to her nape. 'Would it bother you if it did?' he asked, his fingers splaying out over her stomach.

She laced her fingers with his. 'No. I want more children.' She wanted the large family she hadn't been part of.

Slipping his arm beneath her neck, he rested his head against hers. 'Good, because there's something I haven't told you.'

'Oh, yes?' she murmured, not really listening. She felt too comfortable, too cherished, to talk.

'Twins run in my family too.'

He had her full attention now. 'What? They do?'

'Uh-huh. My father is a twin, though my uncle died several years ago. I have twin cousins you haven't met yet. They're currently backpacking round the world.'

'Oh. Identical?' The possibility hadn't occurred to her.

Chase smiled. 'Two peas in a pod.'

She was silent for a moment, staring into the glowing embers. 'They get on well together, then?'

'Inseparable.'

Tasha smiled wistfully. 'That must be nice,' she sighed, and something in her tone reached him. He raised his head to glance down at her.

'Don't you know?' he asked curiously, and Tasha shook her head.

'I told you we never got on. Nat would rather I didn't

exist. She's always seen me as a rival. Someone who takes away the attention she wants for herself. I always wanted to share, but she never did.' There was no point in being bitter about it, but it made her sad and always would.

'That's too bad, sweetheart,' Chase commiserated, easing her around and into the circle of his arms as he lay down. 'I'm glad I married you and not her.'

That could still bring a jolt to her nerves. 'Even though I tricked you into it?' she probed.

'Thinking about it now, it flatters my ego to know you love me so much that you would do anything to get me,' he said smugly, and her heart swelled. It was going to be all right.

'Do you mean that you, a lawyer, condone lying and cheating?' she asked challengingly, and sensed his smile.

'Only from you. Honey, you can lie and cheat your way into my bed any time you like!'

She raised her head and grinned down at his smiling face. 'Are you propositioning me, counsellor?'

Grey eyes danced, and in their depths she recognised his love. 'Interested?'

Tasha lowered her lashes demurely. 'What kind of a deal are you offering?'

Chase's lips curved proprietorially. 'Sorry, no deals. It's a life sentence. Think you can handle the time?'

'You know what they say—if you can't do the time, don't do the crime. Looks like I'll have to plead guilty.'

'Of what?'

Tasha lowered her lips until they brushed his. 'Love, in the first degree,' she sighed, and kissed him.

EPILOGUE

TASHA sipped at a glass of the finest champagne, and sighed contentedly. The sun was shining, the people she valued most in the world were gathered in the garden of their house and all was right with her world.

Or was it? Another glance around the mingling guests told her that Chase was definitely missing. She frowned as she wondered where he had got to. She couldn't imagine that he had buried himself in his study today of all days.

She set her glass aside and began to cross the lawn, intent on hunting him out.

'It went off beautifully, dear,' Elaine declared, halting her in her stride, and Tasha smiled warmly at her mother-in-law.

'Thankfully, yes. I had visions of them both screaming their heads off.'

'Nonsense. The boys are too well behaved to do any such thing. And Chase looked so proud that it brought a lump to my throat,' his mother added, her eyes misting at the memory.

Tasha felt watery-eyed too. 'He loves them,' she replied simply, and just as surely knew where her husband was. 'Excuse me, Elaine. I have to pop indoors for a moment.'

Inside the house she headed for the stairs and made her way to the doorway of the nursery, now decorated in rainbow colours. She paused there, her heart turning over at what she saw.

Sure enough, Chase was in the room. He stood with

a hand on each of the matching cots, watching his sons sleep. On the left Nicholas made tiny snuffling noises, but on the right Matthew was so quiet that for a moment she wondered if he was breathing at all. Then he sighed, and she relaxed again.

This was her family, and the three of them were so precious to her. Chase and their twin sons, who had been christened just that afternoon. It was hard to believe that a little over a year ago their marriage had almost fallen apart.

'I thought I'd find you here,' she said softly, walking to his side, as he glanced round. She slipped her arm about his waist as he drew her close to his side, and Tasha felt her heart expand as she looked down at her sleeping babies.

'I couldn't stay away,' Chase admitted. 'Do you think they know how much we love them both?'

'If they don't now—they will. You'll spoil them rotten,' she teased, rubbing her cheek against his shoulder.

'And you'll let them get away with murder,' Chase retorted.

'Probably.'

Chase sighed, then a rueful laugh escaped him. 'You know they're going to run us ragged, don't you?'

Tasha grinned. 'They'll try to trick us by pretending they're each other,' she confirmed, not having the slightest qualm at recalling the memory of having done the same thing. Chase's love had wiped away her feelings of guilt. The bond between them now was unbreakable.

'But we'll know how to tell them apart,' Chase declared smugly, turning to put his arms around her and smile down into her eyes.

Tasha's hands glided up around his neck. 'But we're not going to tell how we know?'

Chase shook his head. 'Let them work it out for themselves. With any luck, they never will and we'll still have some sort of control over them.'

Her smile blossomed. 'That's wicked, but I like it.'

'Hmm, I thought you would. You have a perverse streak under that beautiful exterior.'

'But you love me anyway.'

Chase lowered his head until his lips were brushing hers. 'I love you so much I can't imagine life without you. Thank you for our sons.'

Her heart contracted on a wave of love. 'You're entirely welcome,' she whispered.

Chase glanced at his sons. 'Do you think they'll mind if I kiss their mother?'

'I don't know,' Tasha breathed, 'but I'll mind if you don't.'

The look they exchanged held all the love they had for each other.

'In that case, come here,' he commanded gruffly and, as she sank into his embrace and returned his kiss, Tasha knew that she had found her small corner of heaven at last.

MILLS & BOON®

Next Month's Romances

♡

Each month you can choose from a wide variety of romance novels from Mills & Boon. Below are the new titles to look out for next month from the Presents and Enchanted series.

Presents™

AN IDEAL MARRIAGE?	Helen Bianchin
SECOND MARRIAGE	Helen Brooks
TIGER, TIGER	Robyn Donald
SEDUCING NELL	Sandra Field
MISTRESS AND MOTHER	Lynne Graham
HUSBAND NOT INCLUDED!	Mary Lyons
THE LOVE-CHILD	Kathryn Ross
THE RANCHER'S MISTRESS	Kay Thorpe

Enchanted™

TAMING A HUSBAND	Elizabeth Duke
BARGAINING WITH THE BOSS	Catherine George
BRANNIGAN'S BABY	Grace Green
WAITING FOR MR WONDERFUL	Stephanie Howard
THE WAY TO A MAN'S HEART	Debbie Macomber
NO ACCOUNTING FOR LOVE	Eva Rutland
GEORGIA AND THE TYCOON	Margaret Way
KIT AND THE COWBOY	Rebecca Winters

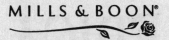

MILLS & BOON®

In Sultry New Orleans,
Passion and Scandal are...

Unmasked

Mills & Boon are delighted to bring you a star studded
line-up of three internationally renowned authors in one
compelling volume—

Janet Dailey
Elizabeth Gage
Jennifer Blake

Set in steamy, sexy New Orleans, this fabulous collection of
three contemporary love stories centres around one magical
night—the annual masked ball.

Disguised as legendary lovers, the elite of New Orleans are
seemingly having the times of their lives.
Guarded secrets remain hidden—until midnight...
when *everyone* must unmask...

Available: August 1997   Price: £4.99

ERICA SPINDLER

Bestselling Author of *Forbidden Fruit*

FORTUNE

BE CAREFUL WHAT YOU WISH FOR... IT JUST MIGHT COME TRUE

Skye Dearborn's wishes seem to be coming true, but will Skye's new life prove to be all she's dreamed of—or a nightmare she can't escape?

"A high adventure of love's triumph over twisted obsession."

—*Publishers Weekly*

"Give yourself plenty of time, and enjoy!"

—*Romantic Times*

**AVAILABLE IN PAPERBACK
FROM JULY 1997**

FREE!

FOUR FREE
specially selected
Presents™ novels
<u>PLUS</u> a FREE Mystery Gift
when you return this page...

Return this coupon and we'll send you 4 Mills & Boon® Presents™ novels and a mystery gift absolutely FREE! We'll even pay the postage and packing for you.

We're making you this offer to introduce you to the benefits of the Reader Service™– FREE home delivery of brand-new Mills & Boon Presents novels, at least a month before they are available in the shops, FREE gifts and a monthly Newsletter packed with information, competitions, author profiles and lots more...

Accepting these FREE books and gift places you under no obligation to buy, you may cancel at any time, even after receiving just your free shipment. Simply complete the coupon below and send it to:

MILLS & BOON READER SERVICE, FREEPOST, CROYDON, SURREY, CR9 3WZ.

READERS IN EIRE PLEASE SEND COUPON TO PO BOX 4546, DUBLIN 24

NO STAMP NEEDED

Yes, please send me 4 free Presents novels and a mystery gift. I understand that unless you hear from me, I will receive 6 superb new titles every month for just £2.20* each, postage and packing free. I am under no obligation to purchase any books and I may cancel or suspend my subscription at any time, but the free books and gift will be mine to keep in any case. (I am over 18 years of age)

P7YE

Ms/Mrs/Miss/Mr_____
BLOCK CAPS PLEASE

Address_____

_____

_____ Postcode _____

JASMINE CRESSWELL

Internationally-acclaimed Bestselling Author

SECRET SINS

The rich are different—they're deadly!

Judge Victor Rodier is a powerful and
dangerous man. At the age of twenty-seven,
Jessica Marie Pazmany is confronted with
terrifying evidence that her real name is
Liliana Rodier. A threat on her life prompts
Jessica to seek an appointment with her
father—a meeting she may live to regret.

**AVAILABLE IN PAPERBACK
FROM JULY 1997**